Skylar Mars

and The

Mysterious

Armada

by Drew Seren

See what Drew Seren is up to.
Visit his website www.drewseren.com
And sign up for his newsletter

Copyright 2018 © MysticHawker Press
http://www.mystichawker.com

ISBN: 13-978-1-945632-27-3

Edited by Cat Lauria
Cover design by Silver Circle Images

1
Unexpected Guests

SKYLAR MARS sat in the copilot's chair next to Philaneo Clawson as Phil's ship emerged from the stargate near Stars' End Academy, the space station where Skylar studied to gain control of his psychic skills. Since leaving Hummassa, the planet he'd been born on, his life had been one adventure after another. Most of them were things he kept stumbling upon, but all in all, he wouldn't have changed them for anything.

"That's not right," Phil muttered as the frantic blurring of light and darkness caused by traveling through the stargate faded, replaced by normal space, and they got a look at Stars' End.

A huge armada of ships was near the space station.

"Shouldn't they have moved on by now?" Skylar peered closer at the ragtag collection of vessels. They'd appeared in the space near the school right before Skylar and the other students had departed for a scheduled break.

"Exactly." Phil tapped his com. "Stars' End, this is Philaneo Clawson on *Rescue Paw One*, please come in."

"What's going on?" Solaria, one of Skylar's closest friends and Phil's niece, asked as she came into the cockpit from the back of the ship.

"There are lots of people scared," reported Filzbalm, the Solar Drake Skylar had bonded to several months earlier. Filzbalm stood tall on Skylar's shoulder, using Skylar's ear for balance. Long talons lightly touched Skylar's skin as Filzbalm used his bright orange

and gold wings to keep from moving much. His neck curved, so he could rest his almost equine head on Skylar's hair.

"Scared?" Skylar leaned a little forward in his seat.

"Phil, are you part of the rescue we've requested?" Ms. Grissom, the school's head counselor asked through the speaker.

Skylar was a little surprised that Phil had put his com channel on speaker, but then he'd done that previously when Skylar was flying with him. Skylar often thought Phil was discreetly trying to teach him things about starship etiquette by example. Being a level ten feeler, it was likely he'd picked up on the excitement that always filled Skylar when he was in space, traveling from one place to another. Although over the past few months, just being on Stars' End and floating around a gas giant on a distant arm of the Milky Way Galaxy excited him daily—it was so much better than being on a planet all the time.

"Rescue? Fiona, what are you talking about?" Phil glanced at the com link and then at Solaria and Skylar like he was thinking about taking the com off speaker but didn't do anything.

"Can you see the armada?" There was a quaver in Ms. Grissom's voice that Skylar had never heard before.

It sent a chill through him, and he realized she was one of the sources of fear Filzbalm was picking up on. He had no idea how many of the students, teachers, and staff had stayed on the station while the rest went on break. He wasn't even sure how early they were coming back from Pantheria, where he and Solaria spent the break with her parents. Of course, it hadn't been much of a break— they'd ended up helping save the planet from an ancient being named Freyandor bent on reclaiming it from the Pantherians and humans who had imprisoned her nearly a thousand years earlier.

"Yeah, we see it. We figured it would been gone by now." Phil tapped a control and the view on the screen zoomed in.

"It should at least be on the other side of the sun by now. The ships are old, ancient, and we can't sense any lifeforms, but they turned and surrounded us right after we pulled our probes back." Ms. Grissom paused. "They've just launched a ship toward us. It's moving slowly. Phil, can you intercept?"

"And do what?" Phil reached up, tapped the screen and enlarged a spot near one of the star ships that was nearly the same size as Stars' End. The spot revealed a sleek silver ship flying toward the space station.

"You've got a couple of movers on board. I know your ship doesn't have weapons, but maybe they can do something. None of the stronger movers who went on break have come back, and Professor Toridon is down with a head cold. He can't move a tissue, let alone a ship."

"A ship?" Solaria sounded a little put out. "She wants us to move ships? Is she crazy?"

"We could link up and do it," Filzbalm suggested as he flapped a bit to land on Skylar's head.

"Is that a good idea?" Skylar asked. The last time they'd linked up, they'd had the crystal claw on Pantheria and used its focus to re-imprison Freyandor. An ancient artifact designed to merge psychics into unified force, the crystal claw had tipped the scales of battle to their side, but the battle had cost Solaria's Aunt Blizza her life. He wasn't sure they should link up to give Solaria the strength to move an ship.

"No, it's not a good idea," Solaria snapped. "Even after several days, I'm still wiped out. Unless we could find some stimpatches, that would help."

"Filzbalm was suggesting we link up and amplify our powers," Skylar relayed, although he was a little worried that someone in the cockpit might think they should try.

Phil shook his head. "I'd rather we don't do that. I don't want us to inadvertently do something that could damage any of you, let alone all of us. Other than Skylar and Filzbalm, who have a permanent mental bond, no linking of minds and powers unless there is no other choice, which means we get boarded, they've got guns, or the station is blowing up."

Relief flooded Skylar. During the final battle with Freyandor, Blizza had been the center of their focus and when she died, Skylar had taken up the crystal claw and directed their power until the claw exploded. Having several people's minds and power in his control was disconcerting, and not something Skylar wanted to do again any time soon. He was too untrained to have that kind of power under his control—even though Filzbalm and the Mother of Drakes had been in his mind with him, it had been terrifying.

"So, what do we do?" Solaria asked, leaning on the back of Skylar's chair and stroking Filzbalm's head. Skylar couldn't see her actual hand moving, but the way the Solar Drake's weight shifted on Skylar's head, he knew what was going on. Solaria was probably scratching his horns which seemed to grow more each day.

Phil fiddled with the controls. "We're faster than they are. We can reach the station first, even if they are closer right now." He tapped his com. "Fiona, have you noticed any weapons on their ships?"

"There's a lot of things that we can't identify for sure," Ms. Grissom replied. "They might be old and slow, but they seem to adapt to our scans, and since the first day they've been able to block us. For all I know, they're blocking our coms out of the solar system. Our messages go out, but we never get a reply."

"Are any of the other students back from break yet?" Phil made some final adjustments and a course appeared on the viewscreen as the image zoomed out from the close-up of the silver ship moving closer to the station.

"No, you're the first. Wait a minute, my scans of your ship are working just fine, but you're several students short of what you left with." An agitated tone entered Ms. Grissom's voice, sounding more like her regular voice than the scared tone she'd been using seconds before.

"I'll explain in a little while." Phil grabbed the yoke. "I can beat the ship to the docking port at the main hall. Meet us there."

"Will do, we'll drop the shields when you need to clear them."

Although Phil didn't do anything, there was a soft click as the connection between the coms ended. A look of grim determination creased Phil's brow. "Solaria, get in the back and make sure everyone's buckled in. This may get a little bumpy if they try to stop us from approaching."

"We're going through their fleet?" Skylar asked as he followed Phil's instructions and buckled his seatbelt.

"I hope all their ships move as slowly as the one they've launched." Phil's hands tightened on the steering yoke. "As long as they don't start shooting at us, we should be fine. Although tractor beams would also be bad."

Skylar had to agree as Phil piloted the ship along the course he'd plotted.

"Phil, do you mind if I ask a question?" Skylar said as they went along.

"As long as I don't have to get up from here, we're good." Phil didn't look away from the main screen.

"I've never seen you actually plot a course before, at least not on the viewscreen like this." Skylar waved at the screen in front of them, that had become a hybrid of the actual view out the glass and the graphic overlay with a dashed line Phil was following.

"I don't normally have to navigate through obstacles like this. There have been times, such as rescues in asteroid fields, or after a ship-to-ship battle where there's debris floating around I had to account for. Luckily, those things don't pop up very often. Mostly it's an easy flight from a stargate to my destination. I've come through the gates we've just traversed so often I could do it in my sleep."

It made Skylar wonder if the ship they'd "borrowed" when they'd tried to take Filzbalm home to Armstrong's Rings had had a display like that. Del, his roommate and best friend, had plotted their course, but the display had been opaque, not a hybrid like Phil's. In his mind, Skylar started making a list of the things he wanted when he got his own ship after graduating from Stars' End and went to work for Intergal Rescue, like Phil. He added the hybrid display to that list. It was a great piece of tech.

"That explains it. Thanks." Skylar settled back in his seat, and Filzbalm crawled off his head to drape across the headrest. Even though Phil had adjusted Skylar's emotions when they'd first met, dulling the effect of Skylar's mother's death until he was in a safe place and could deal with it properly, Phil was normally straight with him, and he appreciated that. A lot of the times with some of the teachers at school, Skylar felt like they were keeping things from him and the other students.

"I've got no doubt that in a few years, you're going to make a great pilot and will be just like me, knowing your regular routes like the back of your hand." Phil turned the yoke and adjusted the ship to follow the course laid out before them.

"I hope so." There wasn't anything Skylar wanted more than to explore the universe. He'd never even considered it before he left Hummassa. Since leaving that backwater tropical world, he wanted to keep going and see everything the universe had to offer.

A blast of red light shot out of the closest large ship.

Phil yanked hard on the yoke and the ship swerved to avoid the beam. "I thought this was going too easy." He pressed the button for the internal com. "Hang on everyone. We're under fire."

"Let's hope they haven't figured out our most direct course." Phil flew erratically as they continued to follow the path he'd set up on the screen.

"Anything I can do?" Skylar gripped the arms of his seat. He never dreamed he'd end up in a space battle, just trying to get back to school. For a second, it felt like an exciting game, until the ship shook when one of the beams passed too close to them.

"At this point, just stay in your seat and hold on," Phil said as he turned the yoke and they dropped down from their current path.

Filzbalm's talons sank into the soft material of the headrest causing the cushion to squeak slightly. *"This isn't any fun."*

"We have to trust Phil," Skylar replied. His pulse was hammering away and he wished there was something he could do.

More beams shot out of the ship, coming from different locations.

Phil opened a connection to Stars' End. "Stars' End, this is Philaneo Clawson. We're taking fire from the ships surrounding the station."

"Then break off." Ms. Grissom sounded angry. "I'll not have those children in danger! Do you hear me, Phil?"

"But the school needs help," Phil objected as he spun the ship away from another barrage coming from the large ship on the other side of them.

"Not at the risk of the students you have on board."

The second ship to fire on them spat out several more ships, smaller than the one that was still flying toward Stars' End.

"Phil, we've got incoming." Skylar pointed at the viewscreen.

A wave of calm and peacefulness rolled off Phil. It was broad, and unfocused. It took Skylar a second to realize that he was hoping to influence the oncoming ships. In one of Professor Aduncus's lessons on using his powers, the professor had explained that feelers like Phil could influence people at great distances, but they needed something to focus on to be their most effective. If Phil was trying a broad range empathic projection, he was desperate.

"Phil, if you're trying to influence the ships, don't," Ms. Grissom's voice came over the speaker. "We've been trying every time they get close. They're as immune to our powers as they are to our scanners. Turn around and get the students to safety."

Risking a bond with Phil, Skylar touched his furry arm and opened up his mind, letting Phil pull some of his power in hopes of making a difference. For a moment, his power drained out of him, feeling like a tugging in his mind. He grew lightheaded. The sense of peacefulness increased even as more shots were fired and Phil continued to roll the ship this way and that.

"Let go, Skylar," Phil grumbled. "We're not doing any good."

"It's empathic and at a distance—how can you tell?" Skylar didn't want to give up. He wanted to give them the edge they needed to get through the ships and to Stars' End.

"I've been doing this long enough. I can tell." Phil pulled his arm away from Skylar, breaking their connection.

"But there's more of them coming." Skylar pointed to the screen again as another dozen or so ships came from the closer vessel.

Phil sighed and shook his head as he pulled up on the yoke. "There's too many of them." He hit the arm of his chair. "All right, Fiona, we're breaking off. I'm heading back through the stargate to get everyone to safety. I'll round up help and come back."

"They penetrated our shields a couple of hours ago. We've cobbled together repairs, but if they hit us too hard again, we're defenseless. We'll do what we can." She cut the com connection.

"Damn," Phil muttered as he continued to dodge the blazing energy beams that came from the larger vessels as the smaller ships fell behind them. "I just hope they don't follow us."

"We're going through the stargate–how can they follow us?" Skylar stared at the viewscreen and the stargate was just a small dot in the distance. It was going to take them a while to get there.

"If they manage to lock the coordinates, they'll be able to use our destination." Phil gripped the yoke as he leveled out their flight. "We should be out of weapon's range, unless they waited until we were close to open fire—"

A bolt of energy hit the ship.

Everything shuddered. For a moment, it felt like the ship was about to fly apart. Skylar squeezed the armrest so hard, he thought he was going to rip into it.

Filzbalm's talons dug into Skylar's shoulder as the little Solar Drake was thrown off the headrest. *"That was a bad hit."*

"Let go!" Skylar did his best to not holler out in pain, but it was the first time Filzbalm had ever hurt him, even unintentionally.

After less than a second, Filzbalm let go. *"Sorry."* The little Solar Drake rubbed his head against Skylar's neck, and the feeling of love and compassion that went through him was so intense there was no way Skylar could be mad at him.

Phil jerked the yoke from side to side and the ship slowly responded, but it wasn't moving nearly as fast as it had been.

"Everyone call out. Are we all okay?" Phil shouted, not bothering to use the internal coms that would project his voice through the ship.

"Fine!" Solaria said.

"Shoulder's hurt, but otherwise okay," Leonada replied. She was the only other Pantherian student from Stars' End who survived their break. She had just told them all she was pregnant as well.

"Hang tight." Phil tapped buttons frantically. "Skylar, check the screens to your right. Anything flashing?"

Skylar turned and looked over the screen that he had no idea what they did. "The third and fourth ones are both flashing."

Phil exhaled. "Great, life support and food services." He punched a button a little too hard, and left a hole in the screen where his claw had hit it. Up until that point, Skylar hadn't noticed that Phil's claws were out. Other than a couple of times back on Pantheria, he'd never even *seen* Phil extend his claws, unlike Solaria who seemed to have hers out a couple of times a day. A lot of the Pantherians at school seemed to like flashing their claws to make points.

Another red bolt passed close to the ship.

"I guess we should count ourselves lucky that the gunners on those ships aren't crack shots." Phil rolled the ship and changed course. "We can't go through the stargate with the life support malfunctioning. We're going to have to find a place to land and see if we can make repairs."

"But we've got to get away from those ships first," Skylar said. One of the control panels he could easily see was the rear-view, back toward Stars' End and the larger vessels. A couple dozen smaller ships were actually closing the distance between them, but the good news was that the bigger ships had stopped firing. With Phil's ship damaged, Skylar wasn't sure how they were going to survive—but if he was going to die, at least, he was going to do it in space.

2
Into The Gas Giant

SKYLAR KEPT his eyes glued to the rear-view as Phil leveled out their flight. The ships were still in pursuit and getting closer. Suddenly, there was a big jump as their ship lurched ahead.

"Okay, looks like I got the engine's electrical system rerouted. We're up to three-quarters power," Phil said as he stopped punching things on his screens. "Now maybe we can outdistance those ships." He glanced around and yelled to the back cabin. "Solaria, can you get suits for everyone? Looks like we've got about five minutes of atmosphere left."

"On it," Solaria called back.

"What about Filzbalm?" Skylar asked, scratching the little Solar Drake's head. "You probably don't have a suit for him."

Phil shook his head. "He'll have to share yours. It should be large enough for him to do that without a problem. We'll just make sure not to catch his wings or tail in the helmet seal."

"I'll be fine," Filzbalm said. *"I'm still small."*

Remembering how large Mother of Drakes had been, Skylar was thankful Filzbalm was still young. They were going to have to work out something if they wanted to keep exploring space. Filzbalm wouldn't always be able to fit into a suit with him.

"Okay." Skylar did his best to keep his attention on the rear-view as the small ships started to fall behind. Since they hadn't been fired on by the larger vessels for a minute or so, he was confident they had managed to get out of range.

Solaria appeared with two envirosuits in hand. "I guess it's a good thing we don't have everyone coming back to school. There's only one suit left in your lockers. I figured you'd have more than this, what with you working with Intergal and all."

"I left a few of them at my last stop in case you all needed more space for luggage." Phil flipped a switch on the main console, then stood. "Skylar, keep an eye out. Autopilot isn't good in combat situations."

"Sure." Skylar kept his gaze moving from the rear-view to the main viewscreen that showed an image of Yeldona Three, the orange gas giant Stars' End orbited at a distance. "So why are we heading toward Yeldona Three?"

Phil straightened from pulling the envirosuit up his legs. "I'm hoping their ships won't be able to handle the atmosphere there."

Skylar's heart, which had begun to slow down after the initial burst from the firefight, sped up again. He swallowed hard. "What? I always heard we should avoid the atmospheres of gas giants."

"Depends on the planet." Phil settled his suit over his shoulders. "We're lucky that Yeldona Three has a non-corrosive atmosphere, as long as we manage to avoid the worst of the storms."

"Not asking for much, are you, Uncle Phil?" Solaria asked as she handed him his helmet.

"I'm a good enough pilot." Phil grinned as he settled the helmet over his head. "Now go get your suit on. I'll help Skylar and Filzbalm into theirs."

Solaria sighed. "I hate these things. I always feel cut off from everything in them."

"I think most species, other than humans, hate them. At least you don't have to spend all your time off planet in a bubble." Phil took the other suit from her and shooed her out the door. "Now go. You've only got another two minutes. Is Leonada suited up?"

"Yes, sir." Her voice came from the open doorway.

"Good." Phil held out the suit for Skylar. "We'll just hope nothing happens in the next two minutes."

"I hope so too." Skylar undid his seatbelt and stood as Filzbalm folded his wings tight and snuggled against the base of his neck. Skylar had been through a basic envirosuit usage class shortly after starting at Stars' End. Living on a space station, it made sense that all the students be trained in their usage, but he'd never had to wear one in an emergency situation before.

He took the silver suit from Phil and shook it out. The legs and arms unrolled with a snap. He put it on like he would pants, then slipped his arms in and pulled it up over his shoulders. Once it was settled there, the suit sealed along the front. Everything felt more than a little big. The gloves that ended the sleeves flapped slightly, like they were made for a species whose fingers were twice the length of his. The boots that went with it were the only thing close to his correct size.

"Don't worry." Phil handed him his helmet. "Once you get the helmet on, the suit will adjust." He stepped behind Skylar as Skylar lifted the helmet over his head. "Get in there tight, Filzbalm."

"This is as small as I can get," Filzbalm muttered as Skylar got the helmet in place.

As he sealed the helmet to the main body of the suit, a display on the faceplate lit up. *Unknown lifeform present. Continue with sealing?*

"Phil...ah, Phil...the suit's detecting Filzbalm as an unknown lifeform." Skylar nearly ripped the helmet off, but they had less than a minute before the atmosphere was gone. He wasn't sure what he was going to do.

Phil rested a hand on Skylar's shoulder. "Is it giving you the opportunity to continue with sealing?"

"Yeah." He didn't want anything to happen to Filzbalm. None of them knew what the ramifications to him would be if Filzbalm was killed. They had to get everything right, but if they didn't get the suit sealed, they'd both die as the atmosphere dissipated.

"Say yes," Phil advised.

"Yes."

A soft click came from the helmet. The suit drew in, perfectly forming to Skylar's body. The only spot that was loose was at his neck and down around his shoulders. The suit had detected Filzbalm and accommodated for him.

Skylar almost let out a heavy breath of relief, then remembered it would fog up his faceplate.

"This is a little cramped," Filzbalm said. *"But it keeps us alive."*

"Yes, it does," Skylar said.

"Yes, it does what?" Solaria asked through the suit coms.

Skylar hadn't realized the coms in the suits were going to override his latest dermal com, which he'd just gotten installed on Pantheria before they left. The old one had been so damaged by EM pulses that he needed to get a replacement. Luckily the tech involved was easily replicated and inexpensive. "Sorry, Filzbalm was just saying it was tight in the suit, but it's saving our lives."

Solaria huffed. "Filzbalm, I'm with you on not liking these suits, but yes, they save lives."

"Same here," Leonada agreed. "I hope this won't impact the baby."

Solaria shook her head. "I've never heard of a suit hurting a fetus, as long as the oxygen mix is right."

Leonada sagged in her seat. "Good."

Phil settled back in his seat and turned off the autopilot. "Okay, folks, activate the gravlocks on your suits. Since the atmosphere in here is toast, I'm going to kill the gravity generator to save on power. From now on, we're on coms and minimal lights until we can make some repairs and get through the stargate."

He tapped a couple of buttons and flipped a switch. A strange feeling went through Skylar. Everything was suddenly light as semi-weightlessness took over. A couple of pieces of mummified food floated up from under the seat, reminding him of the first trip he'd had with Phil on *Rescue Paw One*. Phil was normally so busy that he didn't have time to do much cleaning.

Skylar did his best to ignore the food and studied the screen he'd been watching. "Looks like we're so far ahead of the smaller ships that we're probably losing them."

Phil shook his head. "Probably not. Remember, even if we can't see them, they might be able to see us on their scanners." He reached across Skylar and reset the screen that had been flashing about life support. It became a graphic display of the solar system. Every planet, moon, space station, and ship was visible. "Good thing their shot didn't take out our sensors."

"Wow, how many of these are friendly?" Skylar asked, trying to do a quick count of the ships he could see.

"Anything that's not between Stars' End and the stargate is probably hostile. One disadvantage of being out here, you all can get trained in the use of your powers without having a major impact on developed worlds, is that the station doesn't get a lot of flyby traffic. Stars' End is the only populated center in this solar system." Phil steered the ship straight for the atmosphere of Yeldona Three. "Now, I'm hoping these guys won't follow us in, and if they do, the storms will play havoc with their sensors."

"Is that too much to hope for?" Skylar watched the scanner as half of the ships pursuing them turned back and flew toward the larger symbols he figured represented the bigger vessels they'd come out of. The way his luck seemed to go, just when they thought it was safe to make a run for the stargate, the smaller ships would gang up on them again and they'd be lost.

"All depends on their level of technology." Phil shook his head as the ship bucked entering the atmosphere. "Those ships aren't like anything we've seen. Fiona sent me a message that was waiting for me when we got coms back up on Pantheria."

Skylar nodded. "I remember that. She said the ships were still in sensor range, but continuing to move out of the solar system after they'd been unable to establish contact. Wasn't there something about not being able to find anything about them in any of the historic databases?"

"There was," Solaria piped up through the coms. "We need to have Del look it up."

"Right now we don't even know where Del is." Skylar gripped the arms of his chair hard again as *Rescue Paw One* bucked harder.

Phil had a tight grip on the yoke. "We can debate this more later, once we're in the clear. Let me focus."

No one said anything more as they dove deeper into the atmosphere and the ship continued to complain about the trip. If they hadn't been strapped in, they would've been tossed about like a ball on a Z-GBall court.

Skylar kept his attention on the rear-view and the graphic sensor. The dots representing the smaller ships were getting just close enough to the atmosphere that they could've entered it, but they all pulled up and spread out in a grid pattern, like they were going to try and trap them in the clouds.

The ship's bucking slacked off and Phil sighed as all movement ceased. "Okay. What's it look like? We're in between storms , so we've got an opening for a few minutes at least."

"I think they're setting up a grid pattern, almost a kind of net trying to lock us in here." Skylar pointed to the screen in front of him. The net pattern was fairly obvious, given the way the dots for the ships were almost an equal distance apart.

Phil rubbed his chin. "Okay. That looks very practiced."

Skylar looked harder at the screen, trying to figure out how he could tell that by the way the ships were moving in an almost synchronized fashion. "What do you think this means?"

"I bet they're using a sophisticated autopilot of some kind. They probably got to the point they needed to start their grid and activated the autopilots to do it." Phil leaned back in his seat. "The thing is, I've only seen this in ceremonial performances. Normally in a battle situation, pilots don't like to give this much control over to the computers."

"But we don't even know what species these ships are from," Solaria said, her voice overly loud in Skylar's helmet.

"Right." Phil nodded. "They could be of some kind of hive mind. That might explain the difficulty the readers are having in reaching their minds, and why my feeler attack didn't do anything to them. If the controlling mind is far enough away, we wouldn't be able to impact the drones."

"Which leaves us with nothing useful." Solaria growled. "This is as bad as the hunt we just finished up at home."

"Possibly worse," Phil added. "We're all in envirosuits, and these suits only have a twelve-hour air supply. We've got to figure out something and get moving."

"What can we do then?" Leonada asked. "Can we fix the life-support systems?"

Phil stood. "We can try." He glanced at Skylar. "I need you and Filzbalm to stay here in the cockpit and keep an eye on things out there." He waved his hand at the main screen, which showed the turbulent clouds that were many miles off. "If something—clouds, ships, anything—gets too close, let me know. I don't like leaving the autopilot on, but right now she's got us in a stable location. If we can't make repairs from inside the ship, we're going to have to leave the planet and head toward the asteroid belt near the sun so we can have somewhere to set down. It'll take us two hours to get there, if we can outrun the ships looking for us."

"I'll keep an eye on things here," Skylar replied. "You need to hurry." He wished there was more he could do, but at least Phil had him doing something helpful. If a ship found them, or a storm rolled up on them, they needed to get out of there fast. He just hoped Phil and the girls could get the life support back on so they could get through the stargate and find help to save Stars' End.

3
Blocked Gate

SKYLAR WAS doing his best to not act bored as he watched both screens and listened to Phil and the girls work on getting life support functioning. On the scanner display, the strange ships continued doing a grid sweep of the planet. They hadn't stopped and bunched up like they'd just spotted the *Paw*, which was good, but they continued to orbit in their eerie coordination, making Skylar wonder exactly what was controlling them. Luckily, the patch of clear sky the *Paw* hovered in had stayed storm-free.

"I can't pick up any kind of telepathic communications between them," Filzbalm assured him again, for what felt like the hundredth time since they'd been watching the screens.

"And they aren't broadcasting on any frequencies the ship is programmed to pick up." Skylar kept his reply telepathic since he hadn't figured out how to turn off the envirosuit's built-in com and he didn't want everyone else asking what he and Filzbalm were talking about. It was strange enough that he was hearing everything they were doing in the back as Phil instructed the girls in repairs using their mover skills. Solaria was a more powerful mover than Leonada, and she and her parents figured she'd grown even stronger after overexerting herself recently. They wouldn't know how much more until they were back on Stars' End and she underwent testing.

"Okay, that's looking pretty good," Phil's voice came over the coms. "Skylar, use the panel that's showing the food systems and change it over to life support. Let's see if we can get this going again."

"Right." Skylar remembered how Phil had changed the screen that had shown the life support system to view the rear camera. He tapped the screen that indicated the food system outage, brought up the menu screen, and selected the icon for life support. When that screen came up, it wasn't flashing red anymore. It was yellow. "Phil, it's showing yellow."

"Yellow's better than red." Phil said. "Tap the restart icon on the upper left side of the screen."

Skylar did as Phil instructed. Seconds later, there was a soft whoosh and the life support screen went green. "We're green."

"Good." Phil sounded happy for the first time in a couple of hours. "That means we can go through the stargate. Keep your suits on, just in case our patching doesn't hold. I'm a feeler, not an engineer. I always take her in to an orbital repair port when there's problems."

"That's why you need to find a mover to travel with you," Solaria said. "We're all taught basic ship repair in class, although I think Del would've had things going faster than we did."

"I have no doubt Del would've gotten us flying more quickly," Phil said. "That young man is too smart for his own good. Now, let's get buckled back in and head for the stargate. Skylar, where are those pesky ships right now?"

"They've moved more toward the other side of the planet," Skylar said as he glanced at the sensor screen. "Based on their previous patterns, it'll be about twenty minutes or so before they turn back this way."

"As slow as they are, hopefully that'll give us plenty of time to get clear of the planet and to the gate." Phil appeared in the hatchway and slid into his seat as Skylar re-buckled his seatbelt.

Phil checked several screens, including leaning toward Skylar to glance at the life support display, which was still green with a sliding graph showing a normal up and down pattern. "Okay. Looks good to go. Everyone, hold on tight. We're going as fast as we can. Don't want to risk another hit."

Pulling the yoke toward him, Phil took the ship out of the hover she'd been in and headed back into space. The clouds encompassed them quickly as they sped into the upper atmosphere. The ride got bumpy for a moment. Then they were clear and the darkness of space spread out before them.

Once again free of a planet, Skylar's spirits soared. It always felt good being in space. There were times when he wondered what life would've been like if he'd stayed on Hummassa and never ventured into space. He shuddered at the idea. He'd have been miserable. Sure, he'd had his VR games that carried him to far away planets, but they weren't nearly as exciting as the real thing, and every time he flew in space, he was reminded of how great it was. He never wanted to give it up, not for anything.

"Looking clear," Phil said as he turned *Rescue Paw One* toward the stargate.

"Good." Skylar glanced at the scanner and felt a strange pang at the sight of the large ships around Stars' End. He did a quick count. There were twenty of them. He wished he knew how many of the smaller ships each of the larger ones could hold. Each of the bigger ships was about three quarters of the size of the space station. Skylar had never heard of any civilization being able to build ships that massive. Most of them took too much power to get moving through space, even if it didn't take much to keep them going unless they got trapped in a star's or planet's gravity well. But regardless of that, they were too big to go through a stargate. Totally impractical.

The smaller ships that had been on the far side of the planet broke off their grid pattern and started around toward them.

"Phil, don't slow down, looks like we got spotted." Skylar leaned closer to the sensor screen, not wanting to miss anything that happened.

"Don't worry." Phil continued to fly them toward the stargate.

Skylar was fairly sure they'd be able to beat the smaller ships to the gate—they weren't as fast as the *Paw* was, but they hadn't sustained damage. If everything held together long enough they'd be home free, and once they were beyond the stargate, they'd call for help and come back with enough fighters to free Stars' End.

Ahead of them, the stargate lit up. Where seconds before there were just stars in the giant metal ring, bright yellow plasma began to form, swirling clockwise within the gate's confines.

"Someone's coming through," Phil said as he kept heading toward the gate.

"Do you think it's help?" Skylar asked, turning his attention from the sensor to the main screen.

"Hopefully. Fiona said she wasn't sure if their calls for help were finally reaching someone or not. Stars' End might not be the highest priced psi-academy in the galaxy, but it's still important to the Central Galactic Council. They tend to produce stronger psis than the others do. If their call got through, the Council will send help—if nothing else, an expeditionary force to see what's going on."

The swirling increased and a mid-sized ship appeared in the center of the gate. Seconds later, it cleared the ring and the plasma died down.

"That's a Tursiops ship," Phil said after a second. "See how sleek it looks. Almost like it would be more at home in water than space."

It did look like a large whale, ready to cut through the water with grace and power. "I can see that." Skylar said as he looked at the ship and found a name on the bow. "Looks like it's the *Deep Diver.*"

"That's the Aduncus family ship," Phil said. He tapped a couple of buttons on the far left screen of his station. "*Deep Diver*, this is *Rescue Paw On*e. Turn back. The space around Stars' End isn't secure."

After a couple of seconds, Professor Aduncus's voice filled the cockpit. "Phil, what's going on? We haven't been able to reach Stars' End on the coms in a couple of days but were too busy to check out the problem."

"Check your scanners. The strange armada is back and has the station blocked off," Phil said, keeping their course heading toward the gate. "We've got hostiles on our tail. We've been fired on."

"We'll meet you at the gate," Aduncus replied.

"Do you have weapons?" Phil asked.

Skylar tried to remember if Del had ever said anything about their family ship having weapons. It wasn't something many ships had since most of the galaxy was fairly peaceful, although Tursipia was one of the frontier worlds, on the far side of the galaxy from Stars' End. There was a chance they were armed. If that was the case, there were still too many ships to think about taking on with just them and the *Paw*, particularly since the *Paw* was unarmed.

"Nothing much," Aduncus replied quickly. "A light laser. No cannons, or heavy blasters."

"Then you better hold back at the gate and wait for us to get there." Phil leaned over and looked at the sensor reading in front of Skylar. "These guys are holding tight on us."

"Has anyone tried to stop them telepathically?" the professor asked.

"Fiona—Ms. Grissom—said they appear immune to psi powers. Must have some kind of shield or something." Phil leaned a little forward, looking like he was trying to urge the ship to a faster speed. "They also appear to be blocking communications out of the system, especially if you didn't know about them being here. She said they sent a distress call a few days ago."

"We've received nothing." For a second, Aduncus was quiet. "Del said he's checking all frequencies for any kind of jamming signal. It might take a while."

Skylar's heart jumped. Del was with his grandfather. They had hope. Del might not be very powerful on the psychic scale, but he was smarter than anyone Skylar had ever met. He'd spent part of their break as an intern at the Museum of Space and Time, fulfilling one of his biggest fantasies about being recognized for his brains. If anyone could figure out what was up with the armada around Stars' End, it was Del.

"Good. We've been too busy staying alive to make much headway on things," Phil replied.

"Our sensors are showing your gravity is cut. Is there other damage?" Aduncus asked.

"Food systems are down, life support is patched, I had to bypass engine power, but we should be able to handle going through the gate." Phil glanced at the screens in front of Skylar again. "Life support is holding as long as we don't take another hit."

"I can go ahead and get the codes ready to send to the gate. Where do you want to go?"

"I'm going to send you my Intergal emergency codes, we'll come out at the middle Concordia gate.

We'll be able to rally the troops there." Phil let go of the yoke with one hand and tapped his com screen.

"Concordia…ah…I'd forgotten that Intergal had their central offices in the same system as the Central Galactic Council."

Phil finished tapping his screen. "Sometimes it's best to get in people's faces to get things done."

Like everyone in the galaxy, Skylar knew about Concordia, but he'd never dreamed he'd actually get to go there. There were several inhabitable planets around a yellow star. Most systems only had one planet capable of supporting life, so the multiple planets were a deciding factor in basing the Galactic Council there. It was also near the galactic core, but not so close that gravimetric forces were extreme due to so many stars in close quarters with the black hole that was the center of the galaxy. Concordia Prime held the offices of both the council and O'Byrne Corp.

"Professor, we'll be within the gate orbit in five minutes," Phil announced. "If you could please open our way."

"Of course."

An uneasy quiet filled the cockpit.

Filzbalm shifted a little against the back of Skylar's neck; his discomfort at being in the suit with Skylar was obvious, but neither of them was trying to dwell on it. Skylar just hoped the ship made it through the stargate and they could get out of the envirosuit as soon as possible. They would both feel a lot better, not to mention they'd be safe from the strange ships pursuing them.

"Phil, we seem to have a problem," Aduncus said, breaking the quiet.

"What kind of problem?" Phil asked. "Skylar, are the ships still a safe distance behind us?"

Since they didn't know the exact range of the smaller ships' weapons, Skylar wasn't exactly sure what a "safe distance" was, but they hadn't closed any further. "Yes. No closer than they have been since we left Yeldona Three."

"The gate is unresponsive." Professor Aduncus sounded worried.

"What do you mean, 'unresponsive'?" Phil stood slightly and stared at the main viewer where the gate was nearly filling the image, with the Aduncus ship looking small where it hovered just beyond the gate's normal event horizon.

"It's not accepting any outgoing request." Del's voice came over the com for the first time. "It's acting like there's some kind of virus in the system."

"But that's not possible," Phil said, plopping back into his chair. "The gate system is supposed to be unhackable. Del, check that again."

"Already on it," Del replied. "But we've tried three different addresses so far and none of them are getting a lock. If I can't get a gate to the Galaxeria, then we've definitely got a problem."

A loud chime rang out through the coms. It was so harsh that Skylar wanted to yank his helmet off and escape the noise.

"That can stop at any time," Filzbalm complained. Skylar didn't reply. Seconds later the noise ended.

"What was that?" he asked, wishing he could rub his head.

"Something just tried to take over our systems," Professor Aduncus said. "Del and Melody are working on blocking it, but it seems to have a mind of its own. If I didn't know better, I'd swear it was alive."

"That's not possible, Grandfather," Del said. "We've got it blocked from our system, but as it stands, it looked like the gate to the Yeldona system is set to inward only. Unless we can find a way to break the program that's trying to take over any system that connects to the gate, we're stuck here."

"We've still got hostile ships following us. Any ideas?" Phil said as he pulled back on the yoke and brought his ship to a stop near the *Deep Diver*.

"We're reading ten small ships, probably fighters, behind you," Professor Aduncus said. "Does that match what your sensors show?"

"That's right," Skylar said, wanting to sound like he was being at least a little bit helpful. "It's not all of them, just the ones following us."

"We can't get a reading on weapons," Del said.

"We can't either. Like when we all left Stars' End, the ships are immune to scans," Phil said. "But we can't stay here debating things. We've got to go somewhere."

"It'll take a little while, but let's head to the asteroid belt and put in there," Professor Aduncus said. "It might cause them to break off pursuit if they think we're heading out the far side of the system."

"As good an idea as I have," Phil muttered. "Maybe we can connect when we get there and get something to eat from you. It's been a few hours since we've had any kind of meal around here."

Skylar didn't add it had actually been breakfast on Pantheria and he could definitely use something soon. The envirosuits were great for keeping them out of harsh environments, but they didn't do much when it came to supplying nourishment.

"*I could definitely use some food,*" Filzbalm quipped. "*And if we can get things stable enough in here, we can get out of this suit.*"

Skylar couldn't agree more as the *Deep Diver* took off at a course that would take them away from the pursing ships, Phil following them. He felt better having Del and Melody with them. With Solaria and Melody, he and Del could normally work their way out of anything they'd encountered in recent months. He just hoped a strange armada wasn't more than they could *all* deal with, even with Phil and Professor Aduncus leading them.

4
Asteroid Lunch

THE INSIDE of the Aduncus family ship was a lot neater than Phil's ship. The entry looked like someone had cleaned it until it sparkled. Del, Melody, and Professor Aduncus met them at the door of the entryway airlock. The large asteroid they'd landed on had gravity—however, it wasn't much, and no atmosphere to speak of. But it was providing them a safe spot to get their bearings, since the fighter ships had dropped pursuit once they'd passed Yeldona Three and headed toward the sun side of the solar system.

"We've been trying to raise Stars' End the whole way here," Professor Aduncus stated as soon as they stepped through the airlock. "So far we've not been able to get a response."

Solaria had her helmet off as soon as the door opened. She shook out her hair and let out a loud sigh of relief.

Skylar wasn't used to envirosuits and fumbled a bit with the catch on his helmet even as a feeling of urgency poured out of Filzbalm. Once Skylar had lifted the helmet enough for him to get clear, Filzbalm launched himself off Skylar's neck and circled the lot of them.

"Wow, that was getting really tight in there," the Solar Drake said as he flew around. *"And I don't want to complain too much, but humans can start to stink after a few hours confined in a suit like that."*

"Whatever." Skylar waved him off as he set his helmet on a shelf near the airlock door where Solaria and

Leonada had already put theirs. He wasn't going to complain because the suit had kept them both alive.

"When we first cleared the gate and spotted the armada, I was able to reach Stars' End. About that time, the armada launched a small vessel, similar to the fighters that were after us. When we last saw it, it was heading toward the station." Phil added his helmet to the collection. "That was about the time we lost connection. They had already had one shield breach, but were able to get it patched back together so it will hold, at least for a little while."

"That's not good. By the way, we've got a little food already set out," Professor Aduncus said, leading them toward a compartment with a table and enough chairs for everyone. "We need to come up with a plan. Like you, and from the sounds of it, the school, we've been trying to get a signal out. If the stargate is blocked, then getting a signal through that way is out of the question. A signal going the slow way through the galaxy is going to take way too long to be of any help."

Most of the galaxy relied on the stargates for communication as well as travel. The gates didn't need to open to transmit messages across space. Skylar felt more cut off than he had on Pantheria when the EM pulses had taken out communications. They needed to be able to get a signal out to reach help.

"What about my long-range com?" he suggested as he walked over to the table set up with an array of drinks, fish, and sandwich fixings.

"Unfortunately not," Del said. "Your com doesn't rely on the planetary com systems the way the dermal coms do, but it still uses the stargate systems to get a signal out."

"But if we try to send a signal through when the gate is open, we might be able to bypass that virus or whatever it is," Melody suggested. "Most of the students who've been on break will be returning soon. All we have to do is wait for the gate to open and be fast enough to get a message out. We're far enough away that it'll take nearly a minute for the transmission to travel from here to there."

"So we need someone watching the gate to see when it opens and be fast." Skylar put several small fish in a bowl for Filzbalm. "I can run back over to *the Paw* and get the com." If he was fast, he could do it while Filzbalm was eating, and he wouldn't have to worry about putting the Solar Drake back in his helmet.

"I'll go," Phil said. "You stay here and relax. Do you want me to bring your bag back over, or just the com?"

"Just the com. It's in the front pocket of my bag," Skylar said as Filzbalm started eating. He felt bad about Phil going to do something he could as easily do, then wondered if Phil had locked the ship like he'd done at the spaceport on Pantheria. If he had, then Phil would've had to go with him to let him in anyway.

"Okay." Phil turned and headed back to the airlock.

"Thank you," Filzbalm said with a mouth full of fish. *"This is very good fish."*

Skylar started putting together a sandwich. "I wish there was a way we could arm *Rescue Paw One*, that might help balance things out the next time those fighters come after us."

Already seated, with a fork full of fish, Solaria shook her head. "Uncle Phil would never go for that. He's all about rescuing people. Shooting them would drive him nuts. It's one thing to hunt—we're predators, after all—but that would be going too far." She took a bite of her fish and grinned slightly. "This is very good. Now, *I* wouldn't mind blasting those ships out of space. They're threatening our home."

Leonada patted her arm. "Solaria also fails to mention that female Pantherians tend to be a lot more aggressive than the males. It would be easier for us to defend Stars' End than it would for Phil."

Professor Aduncus chuckled. "I guess it's a good thing we Tursiops don't have the same problem. That's one of the reasons this ship has a laser—that and we occasionally have to deal with pirates."

"Yeah, but our laser isn't going to do much against those fighters," Del said, then swallowed a small fish whole. "Unless those ships are a lot older than they look, they probably have really good shields that would keep our meager beam at bay. Plus, we're just one ship."

Melody sighed. "You know, it would be nice if Mom hadn't been mad about the EM pulse taking out her ship. All of her craft are armed to the teeth. She says it's because we're too important to the Council and any of us would make tempting targets for kidnappers. We won't go down without a fight. I was going to get Clive, our pilot, to bring Del and me back to school—instead, I had to hitch a ride with Professor Aduncus."

"And it wasn't a problem, Melody, you know that." Professor Aduncus took a seat at the head of the table with a plate of fish and a steaming drink.

"I do, and I appreciate that." Melody looked down at the table. "Sometimes I wish I were stronger. Then Mom would care more about what happens to me and let me have more things like my sisters. They both have their own ships and pilots already."

"Don't worry about it," Del said. "We smart kids have to stick together."

The desire to be a stronger psychic was something Skylar didn't really understand—until the Boarisk raiders had killed his mother. He'd never dreamed he might be a psi. His mother had lived in fear of psychics, and he'd been leery of them too until he started to understand they were just like everyone else. There were good ones and bad ones.

Bonding to Filzbalm had chased the last dregs of worry out of Skylar's mind. He'd had no choice at that point but to fully embrace his power. From time to time, he still worried what his mother would say, if she would still love him, but she was gone and he had to forge a life without her.

However, the idea that a parent would judge their children based on something they had no control over, like the strength of their psi-skills, was odd. It was genetic, and although like physical strength, it could be made a little stronger, but if a psychic didn't have the genes for a powerful gift, they wouldn't be able to do as much as a person with the right genes. People like Del and Melody made do with what they had, and both of them were extremely intelligent even if they were fairly low-level feelers.

The airlock opened with a hiss.

"Guess Phil's back," Professor Aduncus said around a mouthful of fish.

Phil appeared in the doorway to the galley. "Skylar, you're a very organized young man." He held up the long-range communicator. "Thank you for that."

"You know, that still reminds me of one my dad had a couple of years ago," Melody said. "It wasn't cheap, and the newer models aren't cheap either."

Phil offered the communicator to Skylar. "Whoever is supporting Skylar has made a fairly hefty investment in his schooling."

Skylar took the com, one of his few personal possessions. He'd lost everything from his childhood in the raider attack on Hummassa. "I just wish we knew who they were."

"Whoever it is, they cover their tracks really well," Del said. "If I can't follow their messages back to them, they don't want to be found."

"And that's something for another day," the Professor said. "Right now we need to work on getting back to Stars' End, and-or getting a message out for help."

"Right." Phil started building himself a bowl of fish. "I took a glance at my scanners, and we're still clear here."

"I've got a proximity alert set in case there's a problem, plus I left Click in the cockpit," said Professor Aduncus.

"Oh, why aren't you guys are giving Fin a lift back too?" Skylar asked as he finished his sandwich.

"It makes sense. And normally saves his family the expense of using the stargates," Del said. "We're lucky. Grandfather's position as teacher and head of the reader program gives him a free pass for using the gates. Fin's family had something going on for the return trip, so we didn't wait for him. A good thing too."

"Sounds like Uncle Phil's Intergal credentials that gets him through the gates without cost." Solaria got up to get another round of fish. "That's why he gives rides to all the kids from Pantheria." She paused and looked at Leonada and sighed. "There weren't a ton of us, but after this break, there's just the two of us. We lost a couple and the rest decided to stay home and help with the rebuilding efforts."

"We're of more use to our people by continuing our education," Leonada said. "Your family is well-placed in Pantherian society, and I'm thankful for them becoming my sponsor at Stars' End." She touched her stomach, something Skylar had noticed her doing a lot since she announced she was pregnant.

"It's the least we could do," Phil said. "You're going to be part of our family now." He looked at Skylar and smiled. "Looks like we're expanding more than we expected to."

A warm happy feeling filled Skylar. Since the Unica family had invited him to come home with Solaria for break, there had been several things said that made him think that he was part of the family. It helped him feel less alone.

"But you've also got me." Filzbalm looked up from his bowl of fish and caught Skylar's gaze.

"And I'll always have you," Skylar replied. He'd been through a lot, but he had a new home and new family, much more diverse than what he'd had on his birth planet, and he was enjoying it that way.

"What's Filzbalm saying?" Solaria asked. "You look like you're talking to him again."

Skylar sometimes hated the fact that Solaria could read the two of them so well she could tell when they were talking. There were times he didn't want to share everything that went on between them. "He's just telling me how nice the fish is."

Professor Aduncus smiled. It was a knowing look, almost like he knew what actually was said, but he replied. "You're welcome, Filzbalm. It was all freshly caught before we left Tursipia."

"I think I could grow to like freshly caught fish," Filzbalm said as he finished off his serving. He sighed and curled up around the bowl. The scales of his belly bulged slightly—he'd had a large meal.

Skylar smiled. It was good being with friends. For a few minutes, he could almost forget there were unknown ships trying to do who-knew-what to Stars' End and that they were all in grave danger.

"Grandfather," a voice announced over the intercom. "I think you need to see this."

"What?" Aduncus got a faraway look, then his eyes widened. "That's not good." He surged out of his seat and rushed out of the room. Everyone followed close behind him.

Skylar wasn't used to seeing his psychic mentor so agitated. Professor Aduncus was one of the calmest people in the galaxy.

The cockpit of the *Deep Diver* was neatly organized. There were five seats as opposed to only four on *Rescue Paw One*. There were also more screens. In the left front chair sat a Tursiops with a similar gray skin tone to Del's. His hair was the same bluish color, but he looked a couple years older than Del.

"How far out are they?" Aduncus asked as he took the right seat and glanced at a screen.

"An hour out, Grandfather," the pilot replied.

Skylar presumed he was Click. Since he referred to the professor as Grandfather, he wondered whether he was Del's brother or cousin.

Aduncus shook his head. "Phil, that doesn't give you much time for repairs. We'll have to move quickly."

"If you can keep an eye on them, let me know when they're about ten minutes out. We'll go get what we can done." Phil pointed for Skylar, Solaria, and Leonada to follow him as he turned from the cockpit door and started toward the airlock.

"We're coming too," Del said. "Melody and I might be of some help getting things done faster."

Skylar handed his long-range communicator to Professor Aduncus. "Take this, in case the stargate opens. Send a message."

The professor took it and smiled. "Thanks, Skylar. I'll also see about plotting several courses. Two will be for escape and one will get us to Stars' End—if we can figure out an opening to get there."

"Too bad none of us are powerful enough movers to teleport there," Solaria said over her shoulder as she rushed down the hall.

"Right," Skylar said. He hurried in her wake. *"Filzbalm, we're heading back to the ship."*

"Meet you in the airlock." There was a flutter of leathery wings as Filzbalm flew to follow them to the door so he and Skylar could get their helmet on and not hold up the others.

They didn't have long to get things fixed. If the armada cut them off, or further damaged the ship, they would be in a world of trouble, even with the *Deep Diver* and her laser. Skylar wanted to do everything he could to get somewhere they could call for help. He just hoped it was in time to save the school.

5
Dodging Asteroids

SKYLAR HELD a wire as Del worked to get it micro-welded into place. They were trying to reinforce the repairs Solaria, Leonada, and Phil had made to life support while Phil and the others worked on different systems.

"I'm amazed you guys made it out of there in one piece," Del said as he pulled the micro welder away from the wire. "All this damage."

"And this was just one shot," Skylar replied. "If those ships weren't so slow, it might've been a different story."

"See, that's what I'm trying to figure out with these ships." Del slipped the welder into its case that lay on the floor between them. "Some aspects of them appear fairly modern, but others don't. I was looking closely at them as we were heading to the asteroid. They all seem to be the same essential design, the basic box, but when you study them, you can see little things that look like they've been patched…a lot. I think they've been out here a long time."

"Here as in this solar system? Why haven't they been spotted before now?" Skylar rocked back on his heels, away from the wires they'd just reinforced.

"No, I mean 'out here' as in space—not even sure which space. There's a lot of it around us." Del stood and stretched. "Sure, the Central Galactic Council controls the known universe, but there's a lot we haven't explored yet. The Yeldona system is about as far on the edge of the Milky Way as we can get. At this point, we don't even know if this armada came from this galaxy, or if it's come across the great empty gulf between galaxies."

Skylar shook his head. "That's a silly idea. There aren't any ships built that can last long enough to make it across the vastness. It would take lifetimes to do that. Without the stargates, travel in our own galaxy is slow as a Marisisan tortoise trying to crawl up a mountain."

"But if their ships were properly constructed, they might be able to survive the journey," Del said. "They might have put their crews into cryogenic suspension or something to help them survive. That could be why we don't pick up any life forms."

"But that would mean a computer is flying their ships and computers can't do that." Skylar stood and dusted off the knees of his envirosuit.

"Actually, they can," Del said. "One of the more interesting things I ran across in the museum is a section of historic text. Lots of interesting information there. One of the best parts was on the AI War that took place on Sol Three right before they discovered the stargates."

Skylar frowned, but he was used to Del coming up with strange things. "I've never heard about it."

Del nodded. "That's because a lot of that knowledge has been expunged from modern history books. So much more interesting to talk about how O'Byrne Corp helped expand the stargate network with the help of the psis. But there was a time when humans had developed AIs, or artificial intelligences. Computers that could think for themselves."

"But isn't that illegal?" Skylar didn't know the reasons behind it, but he did know there were laws dictating what computers could and couldn't do, and it wasn't legal for a computer to be self-learning and self-aware. All data had to be input into them.

"Yes, it is, and that's due to the war." Del picked up the welder case and walked to the next junction they needed to check. "The AIs tried to take over. One of the reports I read said they went after the psis first. The machines got out of hand, and for several years, they fought to take control of human destiny. According to the books I found, they'd decided humans were too destructive to be left to their own devices. Can't see that I really see a huge flaw in that reasoning, except would we all even be here then?"

After the evidence they'd found on Pantheria, that humans had been genetically manipulating people and using them to colonize planets that were too harsh for humans to live on, Skylar wasn't sure if there was a big flaw in the machine's logic either. "So how did the humans beat them back? I mean, they did because we don't have AIs anymore."

Halfway across the main room, Del knelt and started handing Skylar small bags of basic food stores, as he tried to reveal the next junction box. "Right. The book didn't say. It said they were outlawed, and the humans defeated them. But the thing is, if this armada came from across the void, they might not have laws against artificial intelligence. You know, that might explain the virus on the stargate. It really acted like it was alive. If it's an AI, it could be very hard to get out of the gate system."

The idea that something could seize control of the stargate system made Skylar shiver. They could be trapped for years on the wrong side of the galaxy. "But the gate system is supposed to be unhackable."

"That's what I thought, but we can't get the gate to respond on our end. That means the impossible has already happened." Del leaned in close as he opened the junction box. He smiled slightly as he straightened. "This one looks fixed. I think the life support should be fine unless we take a ton of damage.”

“Good,” Phil came into the room from deeper into the ship. “We’re going to need to get out of here. That unknown ship is almost on us.”

“If you got your repairs done, we’re done on this end.” Del stood and helped Skylar put the food store boxes back.

Skylar didn’t say anything, but he hoped Phil had gotten the food system back online. The emergency rations were supposed to be good for a hundred years, but the boxes looked older than that.

“Do you want to go back to the *Diver* before we leave?” Phil asked.

Del tapped his com. “Grandfather, is it okay if I ride over here?”

“That’s fine,” Professor Aduncus’s voice came from Del’s wrist. “I take it you’re all ready to go?”

“That’s right.” Phil said. “We’ll follow you, if that’s okay. You’ve got our only weapon.”

“Understood,” Professor Aduncus replied.

“Del, if you’ll get comfortable with Solaria and Leonada back here, Skylar and I will be in the cockpit.” Phil headed for the front of the ship.

Skylar grinned. It made him feel great that Phil wanted him in the co-pilot’s seat. He wasn’t *officially* the co-pilot, but he liked to feel like he was. “Filzbalm. Head to the cockpit.” He glanced around for the Solar Drake who’d flown off to take a nap while he and Del had worked. As he grabbed his helmet, something told him to keep it close, just in case there was a problem and life support went out again. There was a flash of orange and yellow as Filzbalm flew up from one of the shelves across from the seats in the back area.

"We're moving?" He landed on Skylar's shoulder and wrapped his tail lightly around Skylar's neck like he always did when they were walking.

"In a minute or so." Skylar stopped and glanced at his friends getting buckled in. "Let's hope this goes smoothly."

Solaria rolled her eyes. "We've got how many ships of unknown origin determined to keep us from reaching Stars' End. This isn't going to go smoothly."

Skylar was determined to keep a positive outlook. They were all together, and things always worked out when they were all together, right? He chuckled as he continued toward the cockpit. "We can hope, can't we?"

He got to the cockpit and strapped himself in as Phil fired up the engines.

"Sounds better than she did when we landed." Phil glanced around the various screens. "Skylar, keep an eye on the sensors like you have been. Watch the other screens in case anything starts flashing red. If any of their ships get closer than a few minutes to us, let me know."

Skylar gave him a thumbs up. "We've got this."

The *Deep Diver* lifted off, and Phil flipped some switches and pulled back on the yoke to follow. Several possible courses appeared on the main screen. The blue one was the most direct course between their asteroid and the school. The yellow and orange ones were long paths that went to the far side of the Yeldona and back out the other end of the solar system.

After a couple of minutes, it became obvious that Professor Aduncus was heading toward Stars' End. The large ship that had been approaching the asteroid field was swinging around as if to cut them off.

"They aren't moving fast enough to be a problem," Skylar said.

On the sensor screen, the large rectangle representing the unknown ship shimmered. "What's it doing?"

Phil leaned over to stare at the screen. "What's what doing?"

Skylar pointed at the rectangle that seemed to be splitting into two smaller rectangles. "That." The screen showing the rear-view looked even odder. The two halves appeared to be exact replicas of each other, just smaller than the whole. There were still slender stretches of steel-colored metal joining the two, but they were growing smaller by the second until the twin ships were free of each other and drifting farther apart.

"That's new." Phil straightened in his seat and tapped his com. "Professor, did you just see that?"

"Yes," Aduncus's voice came over the system. "I've never heard of a starship being able to do that. It's almost like an amoeba or starfish."

Del rushed into the cockpit. "What just happened?"

Phil glanced over his shoulder. "Del, you should be strapped in."

Del frowned and crossed his arms. "Hey, the excitement level up here just went through the roof. I wanted to see what was going on."

"The big ship just split into two smaller ships." Skylar pointed at the rear-view screen.

Del leaned over Skylar's seat to peer closer. "Looks like the one on the left is just drifting, but the other one is speeding up."

Skylar leaned closer to the screen. The one on the right was pulling ahead of the other one.

"We're recalculating their speed," Aduncus said.

"No need, Grandfather." Del's brow creased in thought. "If this initial burst of speed is maintained, they'll overtake us in ten minutes. We're going to need to take evasive action."

On the sensor screen, a large asteroid collided with the section that appeared to just be floating. Skylar glanced at the rear-view just in time to see it explode. There was a bright flash of light, when the screen cleared again, that half of the ship and the asteroid were gone.

"Well, at least we know they can be destroyed. But why kill all those people just to improve their chances of getting us?" Del asked.

"Follow us close," Aduncus said as the *Diver* began swinging away from any of the three courses that had been laid into the system.

"Del, go back and get strapped in again," Phil said. "I don't want anything to happen to you." He turned the yoke to follow the *Diver* as she headed back into the asteroid field.

"Why are we heading back into the asteroid field?" Skylar asked, trying to figure out what Professor Aduncus was thinking.

"Click's a mid-range mover," Del said. "Maybe Grandpa's going to have him throw asteroids at that ship."

"We had similar thoughts earlier," Phil said, his voice tight as they slipped deeper into the field than they had been before. "Now get back to your seat, Del—this is about to get rough." He jerked the ship hard to avoid a huge floating space rock.

The floor tilted and Del clung to Skylar's seat. When they leveled out, Del scrambled to get settled in one of the seats behind them. "I'll be back here if you need me." Seconds later, he said, "Phil, you need more seats in the cockpit so the girls can be up here."

"Or fewer passengers!" Phil yelled back as he banked again.

Skylar suppressed a chuckle. He wasn't used to hearing Phil sound stressed. It made him more relatable and normal, not the controlled level-ten feeler he was used to being around.

Filzbalm dug into Skylar's shirt, holding on tight as Phil banked around another asteroid.

"Careful," Skylar warned. "You don't need to poke a hole in the envirosuit. We'd both be in a world of hurt if that thing sprung a leak and we got hit again."

"Sorry." Filzbalm loosened his grip. *"Ride's getting rough."*

"Hang on!" Phil shouted as the *Diver* pitched over an asteroid and he followed.

From what the scanner indicated, the strange ship had just entered the asteroid field. Instead of dodging the space rocks, it was blasting them. Each time it hit one, the rear-view went white for a moment.

"I wonder if that thing has laser cannons on all sides," Phil muttered as he pitched his ship under an asteroid.

"Can't tell," Skylar said, trying to focus on the rear-view and wishing there was something more active he could do. From what he'd been able to see, the ship was shooting the rocks it was about to hit and wasn't bothering with anything around it, but he wasn't completely sure.

Then an asteroid went flying at a high speed and odd angle to the others around it. It was a smaller rock, but it hit one that was a fair amount bigger. That collision caused both of them to move faster. The action seemed to cause a chain reaction. Soon all the asteroids behind them were moving erratically, totally differently than they had been moments before as they smashed into one another. Two larger ones hit the ship hard in rapid succession. It had been firing at the ones in front and not any of the others. The impact with the asteroids sent it tumbling end over end.

Phil dove under another asteroid hard enough to throw Skylar against his seat belt. His head spun a bit. When he straightened, he refocused on the rear-view. The unknown ship had stopped and was floating in space as more asteroids pummeled it.

"To answer your last question, I think it can only shoot from the front," Skylar reported. "I also think it's down."

The com beeped, followed by Professor Aduncus's voice. "Phil, I think we got it. At least it's not moving. What do you want to do?"

Ahead of them, the *Deep Diver* slowed and took up a hovering position above a large asteroid.

Phil glanced at Skylar and sighed. "I'm going to leave that to you, Professor. You're one of the senior staff members at Stars' End. We need to mount a rescue there."

"You're correct, but we need info before we can do that." There was a pause before the professor continued. "It might be a good idea to see about boarding that ship to learn what we can. It might help us rescue those still on Stars' End."

Skylar hoped he could talk his way into being with them when they went. Professor Aduncus was old—he might be a powerful telepath, but he most likely wasn't up to being on the boarding party searching an unknown ship. Skylar had always loved doing that in Galactic Explorers, the VR game he played with his friend Teir back on Hummassa. The game constantly threw hard obstacles at them when they did things like that, and although he knew life wasn't like a game, he was more than ready for his next adventure.

"Let me discuss it with my crew," Phil said, shooing Skylar a questioning look. "We're all in this together."

"I agree. If nothing else, Click and I can explore the ship while you keep the students safe."

Skylar shook his head. "We can't risk the professor like that."

"He is a very powerful man," Filzbalm piped up. *"But like most humanoids, his physical body is not bearing the weight of age well."*

"Exactly." Skylar looked at Phil as the *Paw* settled into a synchronized pattern with the *Diver.* "Phil, you're going to need at least a couple of us to go."

Phil undid his safety belt and rose. "I know. Let's go talk about it in the back."

Not wanting to be left out of anything, Skylar undid his belt and started to hurry out. He paused and lifted Filzbalm off his shoulder. "Stay here and watch the screens. If something odd happens, let me know."

"I will." Filzbalm jumped and landed on the back of the co-pilot's seat, the one Skylar thought of as his.

Skylar rushed after Phil, who was already back with the others.

"All right. Professor Aduncus wants us to go check out the strange ship. I think it's a decent idea since we might find something that will help us get to the bottom of all this and rescue the folks on Stars' End, or put an end to the blockade there. I don't like the idea of all of us going. We're still in a hostile zone. Although the smaller fighters have disappeared, we don't know if they're going to come back. We're not going to be able to watch for them and explore the ship at the same time."

"I can stay here," Leonada offered first. "I'm not a strong mover, and I don't want to put my child in danger if I can help it." She glanced at Solaria. "I am not being weak, I am being practical."

Solaria patted her hand. "I know. Our people have endured a lot in a short time. We need everyone alive. You're not weak, Nada. You're sensible."

Leonada smiled weakly. "Thank you for understanding, sister."

Skylar raised an eyebrow, then stopped himself. He hadn't heard them call each other sister before, but they had been talking about how Solaria's family was taking Leonada and Skylar in as part of their own.

"That's a good idea," Phil said.

"Well, I'm going," Skylar said before anyone could suggest he should stay on the ship. "Filzbalm might be able to sense something we can't, and I can help alert us to trouble."

Phil nodded. "That's a very good idea. We don't know what we're dealing with and Filzbalm's senses are broader than a human's. Del, are you okay with coming? We might need your knowledge, and Solaria, we might need a mover."

"Sure!" They both sounded eager as they answered in unison.

Skylar was fairly sure Solaria was going to see it as a different kind of hunt, where Del never passed up the opportunity to learn something new.

"I can stay here with Leonada," Melody offered. She held up a small portable drive. "I copied a bunch of Mother's ancient texts and can upload them into your systems. There may be something in them that can help us, as long as you send us a video feed the whole time."

"Won't be a problem," Phil said. "We can hook you up with Del." He nodded. "Okay. Let's let Aduncus know what we've figured out."

Before he could tap his com, it beeped.

"So, you've decided," Aduncus said.

For a moment, Skylar wondered how he'd known, but then figured they were close enough he was probably mentally listening in on one of them, most likely Del. From what he'd learned in Psi-Ethics class, it wasn't polite to monitor someone's thoughts without their knowledge, unless Del had given it without any of them knowing. But under extreme conditions, and Skylar was fairly sure the situation they were in qualified for that, they could gather what information they needed from whatever sources were available. He just hoped he'd never be pushed to the point to listen in on other people's minds like that. It just felt wrong.

"Yes, Professor," Phil said. "Some of us will go with you. I'd like to leave *Rescue Paw One* here, so Melody and Leonada can watch for danger for us."

"They can also keep watching for the gate to open so they can try and get a message out," Skylar added, remembering how they still wanted to do that.

"Good idea," Aduncus agreed. "We'll dock with you in a minute and we can get underway."

"We'll be ready." Phil tapped the com off. "Alright everyone, grab your helmets. Del, sync yours up with the ship's coms, and activate video, so Melody can see what you see."

Del undid his seatbelt and hurried to his helmet.

"Melody, you and Leonada come with me to the cockpit." Phil hurried toward the front of the ship. "I've got to set the ship to respond to you in case something happens and we don't make it back."

As they got up and followed him out, for the first time since it had been proposed that they board the ship, Skylar got a lump of apprehension in his throat. There was a chance they would get in over their heads and not make it back, but they couldn't get to Stars' End and they couldn't make it through the stargate. They had to do something. He had to hold to the idea that as long as he had Solaria, Del and Filzbalm with him, everything would work out just fine.

6
Solaria Cuts Into The Problem

THEY WERE all very quiet as they stood in the cockpit of the *Deep Diver*. Skylar watched, a little envious, as Click maneuvered the ship through the asteroids. He made it look so easy. Knowing how much Del didn't like spatial navigation, Skylar wondered if part of the problem was how good Click was at it, but if Click was the family pilot, that made sense. He probably had a lot of practice.

"We're still not getting any signal from the ship," Del announced, breaking the strange quiet that had settled over the cockpit.

"Maybe it was fatally damaged by the asteroid collisions," Click said as he steered them around a large space rock. "These things can pack quite a punch if they hit you at just the right angle."

"It's just so strange that we can't get any kind of psychic reading from them." Professor Aduncus leaned back in his chair and closed his eyes. "We're close enough that unless they have very powerful shields, I should be able to at least get some kind of background mutterings or something."

It was very unusual for Skylar to hear his teacher at such a loss. Aduncus was the most powerful reader many of them had ever met. If he couldn't get a reading, then it was likely everyone on the ship was dead. A chill went through Skylar at the idea of visiting a ghost ship. The thing was, they'd seen it change and become smaller.

Other than that and the lack of psychic activity, it acted just like any ship piloted by sentients.

The large box-shaped ship grew larger in the viewscreen. Everything looked perfectly symmetrical. There wasn't any sign of damage on it. Other than the dark gray color that Skylar took for a sign of age and wear, it looked almost perfect. But he couldn't detect any of the tubes or conduits he was used to seeing along the outside of ships. The exterior was almost perfectly smooth, save for a few minor dings that looked fairly fresh, made by rocks and debris the ship had encountered since entering the asteroid field.

Click shook his head. "Grandfather, Del, if you could both check the physical scanners. I can't seem to locate any kind of access port, hatch, or bay. The skin of the ship looks to be one perfectly formed sheet."

Del and Professor Aduncus bent over the panels nearest them.

"That's not possible," Solaria muttered next to Skylar. "Even the most advanced metal processing equipment leaves marks from where sheets are joined together. Besides that, who would build a ship that you can't get into or out of?"

"It doesn't make sense," Phil agreed from the other side of Skylar, before he could say anything. "We saw the smaller fighter ships come out of one of these larger vessels."

"Not to mention, we saw this one divide a little while ago," Skylar said as he peered at the viewscreen, hoping to be the one to spot something the others were missing. He really wanted to be helpful in some way.

Professor Aduncus straightened from his screen and shook his head. "Nothing. Even the skin of an amoeba has minor flaws soon after mitosis. If the changes we saw in this ship were similar, it should be showing a sign, but there's nothing appearing on the scans."

"I'm going to check for some kind of thinner density in the ship's skin," Del said, tapping his screen. "Maybe we can use that as a way to get in. We do want to get in, don't we?"

"I think so," Phil said. "If we're going to figure out what these ships are all about and find a way to save Fiona and the rest of the staff, we need to make contact. Seeing more of their tech from the inside might be the perfect way to do that."

"On it." Del's fingers danced over his panel.

"We could blast our way in," Filzbalm suggested.

"I don't know if that's a good idea," Skylar said. Every so often Filzbalm came up with a nice, logical solution to a problem, but it wasn't something most humans would think of due to the direct and occasionally violent methods needed to pull it off.

"It might be our only option," Professor Aduncus said.

Skylar stared at him. "Are you listening to Filzbalm and me?"

"Filzbalm is including me in your conversation, not the other way around," the professor replied. "Sometimes you surprise me, little one."

The professor wasn't the only one. Normally when Filzbalm wanted to be heard by someone other than Skylar, he had to mentally shout and Skylar was very aware that it was going on. With Professor Aduncus being as powerful as he was, shouting might not be needed.

"Got something," Del said a little louder than normal. "It might not be much, but there's a section of the hull." He pointed at a small part of the ship that was flashing yellow on the screen. "It's growing smaller by the second. If we hurry, we might be able to deploy the *Diver's* umbilicus to get us attached, then use welding lasers to cut our way through."

Skylar blinked at him. "This ship has a welding laser on it?"

"Most ships have emergency repair tools," Phil said. "I've even got one on the *Paw*. Never had to use it, yet. But if we have many more encounters with these ships, we might have to."

"Bringing the ship around," Click announced as the scene on the main viewscreen swung quickly. "Del, tell me when to tuck in tight."

"Roger that." Del didn't look up from his panel as they drew closer and closer to the ship that was still floating listlessly along in the asteroid field.

The tension in the cockpit grew tangible. Even though they were all good at shielding their thoughts and emotions from others, with several strong psis in a small space, there was no way to block out everything. Skylar wanted desperately to walk out of the cockpit and go somewhere else, anywhere that there weren't so many people. Goosebumps rose on his arms.

But, no matter how much he wanted out of there, he wasn't about to leave. He wanted to see everything that happened. He wished he could see it from the outside as well as from the sensor panels and cameras.

Even Filzbalm was tense as he clung tightly to Skylar's collar. They were dealing with something completely unknown and anything could happen at any second. Skylar half-expected several of the smaller fighter ships to come around the bulk of the larger vessel and start shooting at them, but they didn't.

"Almost there," Del muttered. "Okay, slow down. Don't overshoot." His voice grew louder with each word. "There. Click, stop. Match the ship's movements."

"I'm on it," Click said as he eased off the yoke and hit buttons on his main panel. Seconds later, the umbilicus snaked out from the *Diver's* airlock and got a hold on the other ship's side.

"Come on." Del got out of his seat. "I know where the welder is."

He hurried out of the cockpit with Solaria right behind him. Skylar surged out of his seat and followed.

"Wait for us before you go on that other ship," Phil called out after them.

"Do you know how to use a welder?" Skylar asked as they reached the back of the ship.

Del shrugged. "It can't be that hard. It's a tool." He glanced at Skylar and grinned. "I bet that multitool of yours has one built in. Probably too small for this job through."

"I know his tool has one," Solaria said. "I went through everything it's got on it a while back. Now, just get the full-sized welder out and I'll get us through that ship's hull. Using heavy equipment is part of mover training."

Her statement made Skylar remember that even after months at Stars' End, there was still a lot about being a psychic he didn't know. If people could move things with their minds, why did they need to know how to use heavy equipment? Unless knowing how the equipment worked made manipulating it from a distance easier. That was the only logical thing he could come up with.

Del stopped at a storage locker and swung the doors open. "It's in here."

"There it is." Solaria reached past him and pulled out a heavy case. She grunted slightly under the weight, then grinned. "Movers gotta move." She carried the case toward the airlock, acting like it weighed a lot less than it had a couple of seconds before.

Phil and the professor were waiting for them at the airlock.

"Helmets on, everyone," Phil instructed. "Filzbalm, tuck yourself in like before. We have no idea if there's a breathable atmosphere on that ship or not." He and Aduncus already had their helmets on.

Skylar grabbed his from the shelf next to the airlock, then paused and picked up Solaria's. "Catch." He tossed it at her.

The helmet stopped a couple of inches from her head and then floated into place. Solaria smiled. "Thanks for keeping me on my toes. I can't wait to get retested and find out my new level."

Since they'd gotten trapped in the lava tubes back on Pantheria, Solaria had been pushing her mover powers and was getting more and more powerful. Even without the extra energy of the stimpatches she'd used to give her an extra boost, she was much better than she had been a couple of weeks earlier.

"We've got to save Stars' End before you can be tested," Del said. "So let's burn through this hull and see what we find." He pulled a hand-held sensor out of his envirosuit's thigh pocket and walked into the airlock. "It's going to be a tight fit with all of us in here." Everyone followed him.

"Then everyone hold their breath until it cycles." Professor Aduncus tapped the panel that closed the airlock behind them.

As soon as the heavy door closed, the outer door to the ship cycled and the oxygen in the airlock filled the umbilicus. The ship's gravity also stopped affecting them. Floating weightless wasn't something Skylar had done much. It was always an oddly freeing experience.

Del floated through the thin metal tube the umbilicus formed between the two ships. He held the scanner out and stared at the screen. "This thing is repairing the flaw fast. We've got to get moving or it's going to take forever to get a hole started."

Skylar didn't think there was anything he could do, so he stayed back with Phil and Professor Aduncus as

Solaria opened the welder box and pulled out the big piece of equipment.

"Tell me where to start." She slipped her arm through the shoulder strap and hit a button. "I'm glad these new torches aren't like the old ones that required special vision gear." A blue arch sizzled to life at the end of the welder.

"Me too," Del agreed. "But we might still want to look away as you're using it. There's a chance of things flying."

Solaria sighed. "We've got our helmets on, silly. We'll be fine. Now where do I start?"

Del glanced at the scanner again, then touched the side of the unknown ship. "Right there."

"Got it." Solaria leveled the welder at the spot. "Now, move your hand so I can do this."

"Right." Del jerked back and then walked over to Skylar and the others.

Solaria set to work. It seemed to take forever. Skylar wished she could burn through the metal faster. He wanted to know what was in the other ship. Part of him was worried that as soon as the hole was finished, they'd be faced with a mob of unknown aliens shooting at them, and he wasn't sure if that was a scarier thought than a ship full of dead people. At least he was going in there with his friends.

It was a part of exploration he hadn't anticipated. When he'd thought of going out into space after he finished school, he'd always figured it was going to be finding new planets and helping people, not cutting into the hulls of unknown starships with no way of anticipating what was going to greet them on the other side. He was sweating so much—he worried he was going to need to throw the envirosuit away when he got done with it. He was sure it was going to reek of his nerves and uncertainty.

7
Through The Hull

THE LAST couple of feet completing the hole were the slowest. Solaria frowned and kept at it.

"This is really weird," Del said as he watched the scanner. "It really does look like the ship is trying to repair itself. Like the metal is alive."

Professor Aduncus shook his head. "Metal isn't a living thing. In all of the known universe, it hasn't been found to be sentient."

"Maybe it isn't from the known universe," Phil suggested. "Just because we've managed to explore the majority of the Milky Way doesn't mean we know everything. There's a whole lot of the universe we know nothing about, beyond what we've been able to pick up on ultra long-range scans."

"And we can't even be sure about those," Aduncus said. "With the rate the corps lock down the knowledge that comes through official channels."

With that statement, Skylar thought back to the forms he and the others had had to sign on Pantheria, agreements to keep the existence of the original Pantherians a secret. He knew Solaria, Phil, Leonada, and their people weren't originally from Pantheria, but were a species developed to survive the harsh climate there. They were more human than the cats they appeared to be on the outside. If the corporations were willing to cover up something that large, what else were they hiding?

He hoped that one day he could get Melody to do some digging in her mother's files and find out more stuff. Her mother ran one of the larger corps, even though Melody was a lot cooler than most of the corp-brats Skylar knew. Maybe the corps knew about self-healing metals. Maybe it was something they had developed and never told the general populace about because they couldn't make a decent profit on it.

"We're not going to learn more until we get through this hull and see what's on the other side," Skylar said. At his neck, Filzbalm tried to fold and refold his wings, a sure sign the little Solar Drake was nervous. The motions sent tingles across Skylar's skin as Filzbalm's thin, leathery wings moved the delicate hair at the base of Skylar's neck.

"Then we need to stop this thing from healing," Solaria said as she went back over a spot she'd already cut through that was looking like it was trying to grow back together. The familiar feeling of Solaria using her mover gift washed over Skylar, and the piece of the hull she'd cut through eased out of ship's side.

"Something's wrong," Del said. He lifted his hand up to his helmet like he wanted to rub his head, but the helmet blocked the move.

"What's wrong?" Skylar looked from where Solaria was dragging the metal away from the ship. It was obvious Del was reacting to something none of them could see, or feel.

"He's picking up something psychically," Filzbalm said from Skylar's neck. *"I don't know what it is. I can't feel it, but he can."*

Solaria lifted the piece of hull down the umbilicus and into the *Diver*. There she dropped it with a soft clang.

"No atmosphere," Phil said, as if he hadn't heard Del's stress.

"Let's go." Professor Aduncus was right behind Solaria, and they were already heading through the hole she'd created in the ship.

Del shook his head. "It's gone. I must've been imagining things." He didn't seem too sure about that, but he had a set look that it wasn't going to do any good to debate things with him.

"Okay." Skylar waved for Del to go ahead—he wanted to follow Del in case something went wrong. He would be backup. Even if he didn't have a power set that was as helpful as Solaria's, he could be there for his friend.

Floating from the umbilicus onto the strange ship felt like moving into open space. There was a drop-off from the side of the ship to the closest flat surface.

"Might want to activate the magnetic soles of your shoes," Solaria said through the coms.

Skylar glanced down and she was standing on the wall where she'd cut the hole. It felt weird to see her standing there so effortlessly—then he remembered what a good Z-GBall player she was. Solaria was used to a weightless environment. She knew how to move around better than any of them.

Phil and Professor Aduncus were a few feet from the hole, floating in the openness of a space that looked a lot like the exterior of the ship. Activating his magnetic soles, Skylar flipped into the ship, falling into the darkness waiting for him below. Then his legs jerked, stopping his momentum. It took a second for him to pull himself upright. It was a little disorienting moving farther forward than he should've, but then he was standing next to Del and Solaria.

"Is it just me, or is this place completely empty?" Skylar asked.

"I don't think so," Solaria said. "It would be nice if we had more lights than just our helmet beams. Can't really see much."

"There's only so much we can do." Phil adjusted his trajectory and floated toward the others who were standing on the wall.

Aduncus followed him. "We need to find doors or other passageways." As the soles of his shoes connected with the wall and held him in place with a soft snap, several loud clicks sounded over the comlines. After a couple of seconds, more clicks came.

Skylar shook his head. "Okay, what's with the clicks? Are we having com problems on top of everything else?" He wasn't sure what they would do if the coms went down. Nobody had ever told him how many people Professor Aduncus could link together even in close proximity. Communicating through gestures would get awkward and they'd be almost sure to make mistakes.

"Echolocation," Del said. "Grandfather and I are trying it to see if we can figure out where the doors are. The trick is trying to focus it down through our feet and across the walls. It doesn't work the same way in space as it does in water or an atmosphere."

"Oh." Skylar had never heard of Tursiops being able to use sound like that. But he knew bats and some deep-sea and deep space creatures did. With what they'd learned on Pantheria about humans using gene manipulation to create species for other-world colonization, it would make sense if the Tursiops were derived from a species that had that ability.

"You should've known that," Solaria said softly.

"We need quiet," Professor Aduncus said sharply. His tone showed a level of stress Skylar wasn't used to hearing from his mentor. The professor was normally very calm, cool, and collected. Being a powerful reader made a high level of control necessary. But they were in a situation that had to be vastly different from what he used to. Skylar wondered if he was afraid of something in the dark, strange ship.

"Over there." Del pointed to their left. "It's an opening, not a door. Sorry, but can't tell anything more than that."

Professor Aduncus patted him on the shoulder. "Don't worry. We'll see what else awaits us when we get over there." He turned around and walked around the hole in the wall Solaria had cut, heading in the direction Del indicated.

Skylar followed with the others as they went after the professor. He was surprised by how slow and tiring walking with the magnetic soles activated was. By the time they reached the opening Del detected, Skylar's legs were burning with the effort of lifting his feet while the magnetic field was in effect. Solaria was the only one who didn't look tired behind her helmet's shield. It made Skylar wonder if she wasn't using her mover power to keep herself on the wall.

"Looks like some kind of access tunnel," Del announced as he bent over and peered down the opening.

"It's going to be tight for some of us," Phil grumbled.

"There're reasons we didn't go into exploration, Phil," Professor Aduncus said with a heavy sigh.

"Then you two wait here and let us check it out," Solaria said as she squatted next to Del.

"No, we're all going, or we're all not," Professor Aduncus said. "We're not going to let anything happen to you kids."

"I can go first," Click said, gently pushing Del back a couple of steps. "I'm the strongest mover we've got."

"Wanna bet?" Solaria growled softly.

Skylar put a hand on her shoulder. "Let him go. I bet he can use the echo location trick and without light, that's useful."

She glared at him but nodded.

Excitement rolled off of Solaria—it reminded Skylar of how she'd gotten when they were in caves on Pantheria, and she'd been hunting bats. She was sensing a potential hunt, and Pantherians could lose themselves very easily to the pursuit of prey. Skylar didn't think that would be a good thing in an unknown space ship. She could rush into a trap, or worse.

Click was already crawling into the opening. From the soft sounds coming through the coms, he was doing echolocation as he went. "Once you're in the tunnel, turn off your boot magnets. It's tight enough that you'll move faster without them."

Del followed Click, and Phil went next.

Skylar stood watching them go, waiting for someone to tell him what to do. He wanted to know what was at the end of the tunnel, but didn't want to make Professor Aduncus irritated by rushing ahead.

"I'll come last," Solaria announced. "It makes sense to have a mover at both ends of the line."

Professor Aduncus nodded. "Sensible. Skylar, you go next. I'll follow."

"Okay." Skylar knelt down and followed Phil. The corridor was almost perfectly round; the easiest way to get along it was to grab some of the conduit along its surface and float along. There were spots where the cables were small, and hard to get a hold of. Skylar hoped Solaria didn't inadvertently pop her claws and rip her envirosuit in frustration at trying to get a grip. Then he realized she was probably not even grabbing hold of anything, just using her mover gifts to propel her down the confines.

The tunnel was brighter than he'd expected, but then all the surfaces they'd encountered in the ship were metallic, and the tunnel was no exception. The metal was polished enough for their helmet lights to make the whole area nearly sun-bright.

There weren't any twists or turns in the corridor. It seemed to be straight and flat. Skylar wished he could tell how long it was. He felt like he'd just crawled, or floated, half the distance of the ship or more.

"It hasn't been that far," Filzbalm said. *"Only a few hundred meters."*

"You know, that doesn't help," Skylar replied. He hoped they'd get out of the tunnel soon. Being enclosed was starting to stress him out. He wished he could wipe the sweat off his hands as his chest tightened up, but the gloves kept him from ridding himself of the uncomfortable sensation. Only his training kept him from hyperventilating as he swore the walls were starting to close in on him.

"We're opening up," Click announced. "Wow. I've got no idea what this is."

"Be careful," Professor Aduncus said from behind Skylar. "We'll all be there in a couple of moments."

Skylar wanted to hurry and see what Click had found, but Phil didn't change his pace ahead of him, so he couldn't go any faster.

"Skylar, relax, it'll still be there when we get to the end of this tunnel," Phil said, probably feeling Skylar's excitement.

"Sorry." Skylar tried to rein in his emotions. He'd learned it was impolite to get overly excited in the presence of a strong feeler, but he was just human and hadn't spent tons of time around psychics. It reminded him of how much he still had to learn.

"It's okay." Phil chuckled. "I think we're all a little excited. We've never encountered anything like this. We've got to keep our wits about us. These ships have proven hostile, and we don't know anything else about them."

"I understand." Skylar muttered, but even Phil's light rebuke didn't take the edge off his excitement.

"I think this is just some kind of maintenance bay," Del announced.

"But there's a console over here," Click said. "It might give us a clue about the ships and their builders."

"What kind of keyboard does it have?" Del asked.

Phil slipped out the end of the tunnel, and it was all Skylar could do to not throw himself into the room after him.

"None that I can see," Click replied. "You're the family genius, you find it."

Skylar stumbled as he came out of the corridor. He floated awkwardly about a quarter of the way across the room before Phil grabbed his foot and pulled him down.

"Turn on your magnets again." Phil placed him on the floor.

Skylar activated the soles of his boots again and stopped floating.

"Gotta work on some of this, don't we?" Filzbalm said, reminding Skylar he was in the helmet with him.

"Learning curves," Skylar muttered in return. He glanced around the room. It wasn't much bigger than their dorm room on Stars' End. Along the walls were bays where smaller metal bodies rested. They reminded him of the little lift robot his rescuer had used to raise a tree that had fallen on him the night his mother died. But there were no lights or anything to indicate they were active. There were also shelves of what looked like spare parts, but everything was neatly stacked, like someone had a major case of compulsory disorder.

"Looks like a bunch of service bots," Del said. "Like the ones that clean at school.." He looked at the display screen in front of where Click was standing. "How are we supposed to access this?" He ran his hands around the edge of the screen. "There's no obvious on switch; it might not even have anything to do with this room."

"Why do you say that?" Professor Aduncus asked as he cleared the tunnel.

"It could be an entertainment console of some kind," Del said as he tapped on the screen in each of the corners. "At the museum they had some displays from hundreds of years ago that looked like this. They were simply for personal pleasure. This doesn't look overly modern."

"You think this is some kind of ancient fleet?" Solaria asked as she made it into the room.

"I don't know." Del moved from the console to one of the little bots on a shelf. He pulled at it, and it didn't budge. "If it is ancient, this thing was put on this shelf to stay here."

Click reached around him. "Here, let a mover get the thing off the shelf."

"Don't use brute force," Del objected. "You might break something. We need to figure out how these things are attached."

"I never use brute force," Click said as he wrapped his hands around the bot and jerked. Something popped, and he and the bot went rolling across the floor.

"Right." Del went to retrieve the bot. He knelt down and turned it several times on the floor before picking it up. "That's why you broke its connector."

"Connector?" Skylar clanked over to Del and stared at the cylindrical piece of metal he held.

"Yeah." Del pointed to a spot where something had been forcefully pulled from the thing in his hands. "If I had to say, I bet they use some kind of primitive transference system for power and data. Odds are there was a maglock or something similar to hold it in place."

"But if this is some kind of power station for these things, then why don't they have any indications of being charged?" Skylar asked. There were spots in the metal cylinder that looked like they should have lights.

"Not sure," Del said. "I'd almost say since the ship didn't have any power, except we know it does. We saw it moving through the asteroid field, shooting rocks. It ameoboided on us."

Solaria frowned. "I don't think ameoboided is a word."

"It isn't, but maybe it can be now," Del said, an edge of excitement in his tone. Skylar recognized his joy of new knowledge. Del was in his element, even if they were in a strange spacecraft that was part of an armada attacking Stars' End.

"Whatever," Click said, dusting his pants off. "So you think these things are workers of some sort?"

Professor Aduncus turned from where he'd been looking at another cylinder. "But there are no obvious appendages." He ran his hands around it. "I can feel where it makes contact with the charging station. But there's no current running between them."

"From what we can tell, there's no current in this whole ship," Del said as he continued to study the bot in his hands. "I don't know the answer to that, unless one of the asteroid hits managed to take out their main power grid."

"Maybe it hit something important in that thin area we came through," Skylar suggested. "You said it was growing smaller, like the ship was repairing itself, right?"

Del nodded. "Right." He straightened. "Wait a minute. It was repairing. Maybe it shut down all non-essential systems while it repaired the hull. Once it finished that, things might come back online."

A sudden stab of fear went through Skylar. "And if it comes back online, where is that going to leave us?"

Around them, a gentle hum started up and lights began to appear on the cylinders on the shelves. Then lights from the walls blazed bright.

8
Contact

"THIS MIGHT not be good," Phil said softly as an urgency filled the room. "We should get back to the ship."

"That's probably a good idea," Professor Aduncus agreed.

Across the room, what had been a solid metal wall shimmered slightly, then a line appeared. The line expanded slowly, becoming an opening.

The cylinder in Del's hands shook. The other cylinders on the shelves began similar movements, then popped out of their charging stations. The one Del held suddenly elongated, sprouting limbs and a head that appeared from the seamless metal skin.

Del yelped and dropped it like he'd been stung. It wrapped its upper appendages around his legs.

Skylar grabbed hold of it and tried to pull it off, but it held on tight. "Del, what's happening?"

"I think power's been restored." Del was shoving hard at its metal arms holding him tight.

Suddenly its arms sprung wide and the bot flew up and slammed into the wall.

"Everyone get back!" Click shouted.

"Movers gotta move," Solaria said as some of the bots coming out of their stations slammed back into their alcoves.

"Let's get back to the ship," Phil turned toward the passageway they'd entered the room from. "Well, not that way."

Skylar spun and stared at the solid wall where once there had been an access corridor.

The opening in the wall across from them was nearly human height. The bots pressed against the walls were struggling against Click and Solaria's telekinetic hold. Skylar wished he had some level of mover ability so he could help.

The opening stopped growing. A tall humanoid bot stepped through it and into their room. Its arms appeared to telescope like the cylinder bots' were. Its head was almost egg-shaped, with the point of the chin hovering off the top of its shoulders. Blue, glowing eyes occupied the upper part of the head. Its mouth was four simple lines below the eyes. The edges of its torso were smooth and curved, like its designer was trying to make it appear more human.

It stopped just inside the room. A voice said, "Telekinesis." The voice was neither male nor female. It sounded like a computer using a voice synthesizer and came over their suits' com systems. "So we were correct. Your station is a threat to us."

"You're a robot," Aduncus shouted. "You don't understand threats."

The bot turned toward him. The color of its eyes flickered. "Male. Appears to be a hybrid of human and Cetacea. Most likely middle age. Not the source of telekinesis. You are mistaken. I am not a robot." Its head smoothly turned to Phil. Again, the color of its eyes flickered. "Male. Appears to be a hybrid of human and Panthera. Middle age. Also, not the source of telekinesis."

When the eerie blue gaze passed over Skylar, it felt like a wave of low voltage electricity passed over him.

"Male. Appearance human. DNA scan inconclusive. Also has unknown lifeform sharing life support. Unknown if source of telekinesis. Restrain."

Its arms telescoped across the room toward Skylar. He dove toward the floor, but didn't go very far in the gravityless room. He still had his mag soles on and his overall movement was clunky. He wished he had more zero-g experience, and vowed to get Solaria to teach him all about Z-GBall once they got back to the academy.

"Stop!" Del shouted.

For a second, everything in the room went still. The bot in the doorway froze with its arms halfway across the space to Skylar. The smaller bots against the walls stopped moving. A strange quiet came over them all.

"What just happened?" Skylar asked as he straightened from the awkward half-fall he'd found himself in. When Del shouted, there'd been a kind of energy that hit Skylar—it was similar to psychic energy, but not like any he'd been exposed to before. Del was a low-level feeler, and as his roommate, Skylar was used to the feel of his power.

"I don't know." Professor Aduncus pushed lightly against the metal arm stretched between the thing in the doorway and Skylar. He glanced at Del. "Any ideas, Del?"

"There's a pressure." Del's voice was tight and strained. "I'm pushing against it, but it wants to hurt Skylar and I don't want to let it." He shook slightly. "I don't know how I'm doing this, or even what I'm doing."

"It's like you're controlling the machine," Phil said. "Professor, have you ever heard of a psi who could control machines?" He pushed against the thing floating in the hole it had come through. It didn't move; like it was held to the floor with magnets. He shoved one of the arms, which bent easily along the extendable joints. "This is too weird. Even a human under telepathic control isn't this easy to manipulate."

"Del, can you get it to move out of the way of the door?" Click bumped his hand against his helmet like he was just trying to wipe the sweat from his brow.

"I don't know. I don't know if I'm doing something or not." Del frowned and closed his eyes. Confusion and fear emanated from him, then Del's eyes flashed opened. "So much information. It's like plugging into a computer or something." He sighed. "I guess I was. It's strange. Almost like feeling emotions, but more complex, more detailed."

"A form of machine telepathy?" Professor Aduncus walked over and started to put his hand on Del's shoulder, then stopped.

"Maybe. But this one, actually all of these, seem to be connected somehow. Like they are all one system." He closed his eyes again and the little ones fell to the floor. "Nope, that's not it. It's really complicated. And it's fighting me. It knows I'm in its system. It's afraid. How can a machine be afraid?" Then the big one moved out of the way with jerky steps. "Got it." Del grinned and opened his eyes. "I don't think there's anything alive on this ship, other than us. It's all run by computer."

"Can you keep it turned off until we can reach the ship?" Phil asked, stepping toward the portal the robot had come through.

Del shrugged. "I don't know. It wants me out of its circuits. It feels like someone trying to resist a feeler manipulating it."

"'Cause that's what you're doing," Solaria said. "You're manipulating it."

"Can you find out why they're here?" Professor Aduncus asked. "From the sound of it, it knows what humans are, and what psychics can do."

"I don't think so." Del shook his head. "It's trying to force me out. If it breaks free of my hold, it's going to come after us. It's angry. It's a machine. But, machines can't be angry, can they?"

"Click, I need you to carry Del as we head back to the ship. Be careful not to jar him too much." Professor Aduncus waved for Phil to continue through the door. "Del, don't talk unless you have to. Concentrate on holding it at bay. Keep it contained until we can get back to the ship. Solaria, Skylar, come along."

They hurried down the corridor on the other side of the opening. Even though they were heading away from their ship, it was the only way the corridor went.

"I might be able to boost Del's power," Filzbalm said. *"I'll have to focus on him."*

"Do it," Skylar replied, hoping the Solar Drake was correct and he could help. If the machines on the ship were going to try to secure Skylar, and probably the others too, they needed every possible edge to get off the ship and back to the school. "Filzbalm is going to see if he can help Del."

Skylar's hand grew warm. He went to scratch it, but the suit's gloves prevented the move. Then he remembered the chip of the crystal claw that had embedded itself in his hand. The artifact had allowed him and his friends to link their minds together to defeat a frozen original inhabitant on Pantheria. He hadn't mentioned it to anybody, as the wound had healed almost as fast as it had formed when the crystal pierced his skin. But as it burned while Filzbalm reached out to Del, Skylar wondered if the shard was more than he had thought at the time.

They reached an intersection. Phil glanced both ways, then went left.

"Why are we going this way?" Skylar asked as they hurried down a metal hallway that looked identical to the other one.

"Fastest way to the ship," Solaria responded.

"And he knows this how?" Skylar hadn't seen Phil consult a sensor or anything.

Solaria sighed heavily. "He's a predator like me, silly."

Sometimes Skylar really wished she'd come up with another answer to questions. He didn't say anything as they continued, then made another turn. It felt like they'd been going for a long time.

"Hey," Melody called over the coms. "Somebody came through the stargate. We got a message off."

"Can you tell who it was?" Professor Aduncus said. "Contact them. Tell them to not head to the school, but to come to us."

"Professor, that might not be a good idea," Phil said as they made another turn down a hall that looked like all the others. "We'll be leading those fighter ships right to us."

"What else can we do?" Professor Aduncus snapped. "If they're students, they'll be in danger."

"It's the Cosmos's ship," Melody said. "They've got full weapons." She chuckled. "Never thought their paranoia would be a good thing."

"Weapons might help us out," Phil said. "Okay. Tell them where we are. We'll be back on board soon." They made another turn and entered a huge room.

Phil paused and stared around. "We should be there."

The walls of the room were the same shiny metal as the rest of the ship. With basic lighting on, it was possible to see across the room. The place was immense, easily twice the size of the cafeteria at Stars' End. There were several openings on different levels of the walls, and one of them looked like a ragged rip that was slowly resealing.

"Is that our way out?" Skylar pointed to the tear that was getting smaller by the second.

"Del, stop the ship from repairing itself!" Solaria shouted.

"Easier said than done." Del sounded scared and far away.

"The machine intelligence is gaining an upper hand," Filzbalm said, sounding more tired than Skylar had heard him sound in a while.

"What can we do?" Skylar asked. There was nothing in the room they could use to hold the gap open, and even if they could, it wasn't big enough for any of them other than Filzbalm to get through.

"Did you bring your multitool?" Solaria asked, running up the wall.

Skylar checked the leg pocket of his suit. "Here." He tossed it at her.

The tool tumbled end over end in the lack of gravity, then changed course and landed in her hand as she continued up the wall toward the tear. She flipped the tool open and seconds later a small laser torch blazed in her grip. She set to work re-cutting the hole that would take them into the umbilicus as the rest of them made it up the wall to her.

"Work fast," Del muttered. "I'm on defense now and I don't know how long I can hold it back."

"Trying," Solaria said as she finished the second side of the door, then sighed. "No time for pretty." She cut an arch instead of a straight line. "Not like this damned ship isn't going to repair itself anyway."

"Solaria." Phil growled.

"What?" She continued cutting.

Del began thrashing in Click's telekinetic hold.

"It's breaking free," Filzbalm said and fear surged through their connection.

Skylar closed his eyes and pushed his own strength out to the Solar Drake and hoped he pass it on to Del. He remembered what it had felt like when he'd become the focus for the linked mind gestalt the crystal claw had formed between them. The chip of crystal under his skin burned with power.

After a couple of seconds, Skylar started feeling light-headed, but Del and Filzbalm were there with him. The three of them were surrounded by something. It was like being in Professor Aduncus' mind during training exercises, but more vast, more focused.

"Get out!" it screamed at them. A torrent of power flashed over them. It tingled like the bots scans had.

"No!" Del shouted. The power flowed from Skylar, through Filzbalm and the crystal to Del. Skylar felt Del shove back at the machine intelligence. It gave way as if it hadn't expected Del's renewed assault.

"We've got this!" Skylar shouted as he fought the sudden lightheadedness from the psychic engery drain and focused all his power on Del.

Del caught the power and shoved it at the machine mind as hard as he could. The entire vessel shook.

"What happened to the lights?" Solaria asked.

Skylar opened his eyes. The big room was as dark as it had been when they came in from Phil's ship. Their attack on the machine had an effect on the physical form of the ship. Skylar had read the theories on how a telepath could shut down another's mind. He tried to remember how it worked and feed that information to Del.

"Try this."

"But that's for a normal mind—this isn't organic, and I'm not a telepath," Del objected.

"No, but you're holding this thing at bay. You're having an impact on how it powers the ship. Let's try and shut it down for good." Skylar pushed more power to Del as he sent the information at him. The basics of the attack were fairly brutal, and if a telepath wasn't careful, they could do permanent damage to the mind they hit. There

was no safe way to practice the technique and any reader who wasn't either being attacked in a life or death situation, or under the direct orders from a government official to attack a mind in such a way, would be imprisoned for abuse of power. But he didn't think such restrictions applied to a machine mind and even if it did, they had been attacked.

"Okay, let's try this." Del gathered up the power Skylar and Filzbalm were pushing at him.

"We can do this," Filzbalm added.

The power roared through them, and Del struck at the intelligence that was trying to gather its focus.

"Got it!" Solaria shouted. "Get moving."

Skylar staggered as he jerked his eyes open. Trying to interact with the physical world while helping Del in the mental one was too much. Everything spun around him. He barely felt Phil catch him as he fell.

The machine's scream of agony reverberated through him as Phil lifted him and hauled him through the hole Solaria had cut. It was like nothing Skylar had ever heard before. It tore at him. He never intended to cause anything harm. He'd been defending himself and the others.

At some point, Del started screaming too, and his cries of pain merged with the machine's. Then they both went quiet and darkness encompassed Skylar.

9
Pondering Intelligence

"IT"S STILL not repairing the hole." Solaria's voice woke Skylar.

He was lying on the couch in the *Deep Diver*. Filzbalm was curled up on his chest, snoring softly. The Solar Drake was tired, but otherwise okay.

"Maybe it's really dead this time?" Melody suggested from the *Paw*. She and Leonada were staying in contact with the others through open coms.

"I don't know," Phil said. "Maybe we'll know more when Del wakes up. He handled the brunt of the attack."

"He's not awake yet?" Carefully picking up Filzbalm, Skylar started to get up, but his head spun violently, and he eased himself back down.

"Take it easy." Phil put a hand on Skylar's shoulder. Calming emotions rolled off Phil.

Skylar didn't bother fighting them. He was wasted after helping Del defeat the machine intelligence. His throat was dry and his stomach rumbled.

"I could eat too," Filzbalm said softly, then uncurled from Skylar's hands and flew to the table.

"Here." Phil handed him a cup of water. "Take it easy. I'll get you something from the food generators. Something for Filzbalm too."

"Thanks." Skylar eased himself into a seated position. He wanted to get up and do something, but his body was weak. He'd pushed himself before. He'd seen Solaria pushed to the breaking point. He needed to get some food in him and rest more before his mental powers were going to be any good.

The water was cool and refreshing. It took some of the dryness out of Skylar and made him feel a little better.

"The Cosmos's ship is about an hour out," Leonada's voice came through the coms connecting them with the *Paw*. "They made it past the armada around the school with only minor damage from the fighters. They took out a good number of the smaller ships."

"What about the school?" Phil asked. "How are they faring?"

"Not well. It looks like the armada has launched a full-scale assault on the school." She glanced from Skylar to where Del lay on one of the other couches. "At the moment, the academy's shields are holding, but they can't mount an offense unless our message got through and help is on the way."

"We can only hope," Phil replied.

"Stars' End was designed to withstand a major assault," Professor Aduncus announced, coming in from the cockpit. "We aren't sure she can hold out for as long as these ships can fire though. I wish we'd gained more information on that ship, or that Del would wake up." He knelt next to the couch where Del lay. "It's like his mind has retreated to repair itself." He put a hand on Del's forehead like a parent checking a child for fever. "He's far away. I don't know what he's done to himself. I would almost say he's developing a new psychic talent."

"If the way he was fighting that machine mind is any indication, I'd say it's that." Skylar set his cup down. "We forced it back using telepathic assault theory. One of the ones you had me study."

"But that shouldn't have worked on a machine, unless it was somehow sentient, and that's not possible." Aduncus lowered himself to the floor and put his back to

Del's couch. "Artificial intelligence has been outlawed as impractical."

That didn't sound right, although Skylar did remember something about that in history texts. And Del had said something about it earlier, he just couldn't remember exactly what. There was too much going on. "Why would they outlaw something that was impractical? That doesn't make much sense."

Phil turned from the food dispenser with a plate of meat in his hand. "Skylar, in case you haven't noticed, just because something is impractical doesn't mean the government isn't going to take steps to pass laws about it. But I wonder if the corporations didn't decide it was something they wanted control over, or maybe it was something they couldn't control, so they outlawed it."

"It was worried about us movers," Solaria said. "Like we were a danger to it. Maybe that has something to do with it."

Phil carried the food over to Skylar. "Possibly. That might also be why machine intelligence was outlawed. If the corps couldn't control it, then ban it. Remember, a lot of the corps are run by the ultra-powerful psis like Cafpar O'Byrne. If there was some lifeform they'd have trouble controlling, then they'd probably want it destroyed."

"Like they tried to do to Freyandor, the ancient on Pantheria," Skylar said as he picked up a piece of the meat Phil had given him. He wasn't sure what the meat was supposed to be, but seeing as it came out of the food dispenser, he wasn't worried about it. There had been a few things he'd eaten on Pantheria that were a little questionable, but he'd trusted Solaria and her mother not to poison him.

"Exactly." Phil headed back to the dispenser for more food. "We've always known the corps hide what they didn't like, or anything they found inconvenient. There must be more to these machine intelligences than we know. They've obviously encountered humans before. It's possible they know about our origins."

"It referred to us as hybrids." The professor took the plate Phil handed him. "The only way it could know that is if it was familiar with both original species. It's been many centuries since the non-human parts it referred to have been around. Some think all the species that rose up on Sol Three died, except humans. The tales are that the planet was nearly dead before humans, O'Byrne Corp specifically, found the technology needed to leave the home world."

"And O'Byrne Corp's history is well documented," Phil said. "The victors always write the history books."

Del moaned, rolled slightly, but didn't wake.

"But this doesn't help us." Phil came over with more food. "Right now we're faced with foes we have no way to fight. Even with the Cosmos's ship having weapons, it's one ship against an armada. The light laser we've got on the *Diver* won't help much, and the *Paw* is only good for running and rescue. We need to come up with a plan."

"If we are right and Del has discovered a new power, or rediscovered one—" Aduncus licked his fingers after he finished a bite of meat "—he might be the key to this. I wish we had more psis who could take control of machines. What we discovered on the ship does explain why none of the telepaths from the school were able to reach a lifeform on the armada. If there are any traditional minds on those vessels, we'd know by now.

"I've been in telepathic contact with Ms. Grissom and she says she and the others who stayed on the station have been trying and not reached anything. She is searching the school's historic database for information on machine intelligences and ways to defeat them."

"Grandfather." Click's voice came from the coms. "The *Nubul's Gold* is nearly here and they've got a couple of fighters on their tail."

Aduncus glanced at Phil. "That could be a problem, unless we can use the asteroid trick again."

"Might be worth a shot." Phil glanced toward Solaria. "Go up and lend Click a hand."

"I'll contact the Cosmos and see what talents they have on board." Aduncus stood. "If they have a strong mover or two that might help even the odds, at least in this case. Might even help get us to Stars' End."

Skylar realized that with several strong movers working together, they might be able to move a really large asteroid that could damage even the largest of the ships. The problem was, as they saw with the one he and Del had defeated, they could fix themselves. They had to shut down the mechanical minds controlling the ships. He wondered if since it was a new talent, if it was something Del could teach him. Maybe other people than Del had the genes for the gift.

The problem with that line of thinking was none of them had any idea how far the talent reached. Del had been within the ship when he was first able to control it. They might have to be so again, and getting in and out of the ship had been the hard part, even with the ship so damaged it had powered down to do repairs. He really hoped the message Melody and Leonada sent had gotten through. That was their best chance to get out of the mess and back to Stars' End in one piece.

He finished the food Phil had brought him and set the plate on the table where Filzbalm was gulping down chunks of raw meat, or as close as the food dispenser could make.

"Where are you going?" Phil asked as Skylar turned in the direction the others had gone.

"To the cockpit. I want to watch what's happening. I'll do my best to stay out of the way."

"I'll let everyone know if…when Del wakes up." Phil took a seat at the table. "Not much I can do up there." A distinct feeling of inadequacy came off Phil.

Skylar paused and looked at Phil who was slumped at the table. He always viewed Phil as a strong, resilient person. But he looked tired and out of place in a ship that wasn't his, where he wasn't able to do much to help. Skylar understood how he felt. He wanted to be more active too, but there wasn't much he could do not being a mover. They were still working their way back to the *Paw*, and would reach it about the same time as the *Gold* reached them. Maybe he'd feel better back on his own ship. Skylar knew if he had a ship—any ship—he'd feel better on it than he did as only a passenger. He'd, at least, have something to do.

"Phil," Skylar said as he walked back toward the table. "We've all got our jobs to do, right?"

Phil shrugged. "Yes. I'm just not used to being in the middle of a conflict. Intergal Rescue comes in when the fighting's over, not when it's just beginning. I'm used to being the rescue squad, not the one needing rescue."

It hurt seeing Phil like that. Skylar nodded—he couldn't really think of much he could do. "All we can do is our best. That's what my mother always said. We're going to do everything we can to get to the station and save the people there. At least we know their shields are holding out right now."

"Hang on!" Solaria shouted through the coms. "We're heading deeper into the asteroid field again."

The *Diver* pitched to the side. Skylar grabbed hold of the table. Filzbalm took to wing as his empty food bowl slid to hit the short rail at the table's edge designed to keep things from falling off in all but the most extreme maneuvers.

Excitement rolled out of the cockpit from Solaria and Click. The feeling made Skylar want to be up there watching on the main screen with them. He was torn between staying with Phil and Del, and going up front to watch the action.

"Go on," Phil urged. "I know you want to. Go up to the cockpit—we'll be fine." He was heading over to the couch where Del lay. Flipping open a panel in the arm closest to Del's head, he touched something Skylar couldn't see, but a cushioned rail lifted from the front of the couch. It was tall enough to hold Del on the couch unless they did some rolls through the space rocks.

Skylar didn't need to be told twice. "Thanks." He pushed off the table and rushed toward the short corridor that would take him to the cockpit. There were small handles there. He managed to grab one as the ship pitched in the other direction.

Filzbalm landed on his shoulder and wrapped his tail around Skylar's neck. *"I'm lucky I finished my food before this started. It would be hard to eat with the ship rocking like this."*

"Yes, it would," Skylar agreed as he worked his way down the passageway.

The ship rocked again. Skylar knew Phil hadn't flown that dramatically through the asteroids before, and wondered if Click or Solaria was doing something to them to get the fighters off the Cosmos' tail and keep from being spotted. The excitement from the cockpit grew stronger the closer Skylar got, and he couldn't tell if it was from his own need to make it up there and see what was going on, or their emotions, but his pulse was fast and his hands were sweaty. He almost wished he still had his gloves on so his hands would stop slipping on the handles he grabbed to keep his feet as the ship rocked from side to side.

He made it to the cockpit as a huge asteroid filled the viewscreen. Click flew straight at it and, at the last second, neatly skimmed a few hundred meters from its surface.

"You're really good at this," Solaria said as they leveled out enough for Skylar to get into the chair next to her.

"Practice," Click said. "I really wanted to go into the Galactic Council Defense Fleet, but they don't take Tursiops."

"And the family needed him on the fish farm," Professor Aduncus said. "We can always use a strong mover."

"Anyway, I love flying and haven't had this many combat maneuvers in real life—just a simulator." He kept their flight tight around the asteroid like he was using it for cover.

"The *Gold* should be just on the other side," Solaria said, glancing at a panel on her left.

"But where are the fighters?" Skylar asked.

"They managed to take out one before they reached the asteroid field," Professor Aduncus said. "But they have three more after them."

"Here we go again," Click said, and yanked the yoke to the side.

The ship jerked away from the asteroid. They were suddenly joined by another ship that Skylar didn't recognize, but wasn't one of the strange fighters.

"We're ready to push," Connor Cosmo's voice came over the coms. Connor was one of Skylar's other dorm roommates.

"Hold her steady, Grandfather." Click took his hands off the yoke and closed his eyes.

The tingle of a mover using their gifts filled the cabin. After their adventure on Pantheria, Skylar didn't think he would ever forget the sensation of Solaria using her talents in the tunnels under the planet.

Then the asteroid they'd just flown over moved contrary to its original orbit. It hurled toward another asteroid as two of the enemy fighter ships came into view.

Skylar held his breath as the two asteroids hurled toward each other, coming together in a mad crash. The pair of ships caught between them didn't have time to get out of the way. They were crushed between the giant rocks. The collision changed the asteroids' trajectory and they rolled together for a distance, spitting out pieces of metal in their wake.

"Yeah!" Click fist pumped before taking the yoke back. "*Gold*, this is *Diver*. We've got one more in this group."

"If you provide us cover, we'll just take them out. Our main guns have proven successful against them so far," Connor replied.

"We can do that." Click looked over his shoulder at Solaria. "Cover's yours if you think you can do it."

Solaria huffed. "Of course I can do it. Which one would you like to use for cover?"

Click looked around for a moment. "That one." He pointed to a mid-sized rock that was big enough to hide the space ship, but not so unwieldy that Solaria wouldn't be able to move it.

She nodded. "Ready when you are, *Gold*."

"We're moving into position now," Connor replied.

"Where's the third fighter?" Skylar asked, peering over Professor Aduncus' shoulder at a screen similar to the one he'd watched on Phil's ship. It showed a graphic representation of the battlefield.

"Right there." Professor Aduncus pointed at a red dot on the screen. It wasn't very far away. If they were wrong about their ploy, it would be close enough to fire on either of the two ships. It wasn't near to any asteroids.

The *Gold*, represented by a bright yellow dot, slipped behind an asteroid as the space rock began drifting counter to the direction it had been.

Skylar glanced at Solaria, who had her eyes closed as mover energy flowed off her. Watching her move an asteroid that was millions of times heavier than the ball they used in Z-GBall made him wonder if she would've been able to do this before they'd been trapped underground on Pantheria. The experience had changed her—strengthened her.

It made him wonder what he'd be capable of as he pushed himself harder, but he wasn't sure how to push his feeler and reader skills. Sure, he could keep practicing with the professor, but there had to be something more— some other way to get better. Something like what Solaria had accomplished.

"Easy does it," Click said, drawing Skylar's attention back to the scene unfolding before them.

Skylar kept glancing between the graphic display and the viewscreen. The mid-sized asteroid with the *Gold* behind it eased its way out of the asteroid cluster and headed toward the open area, where the fighter flew an erratic zig-zag pattern like it was trying to find them all. As the asteroid grew closer, the fighter stopped its odd pattern and hovered, facing the asteroid.

"It's trying to figure out what to do," Skylar said.

"I think so," Professor Aduncus agreed. "That really does suggest more than a basic computer running the thing. It's actually learning from our tactics."

"That means they're sentient, doesn't it?" Skylar said.

"Technically, yes." The professor tapped his screen, zooming in since the asteroid and the *Gold* were close enough to the fighter.

Skylar didn't like the idea that he and Del might have killed a sentient being. It was true that he wanted to take vengeance on the Boarisk for what they'd done to his home planet of Hummassa and his mother, but the Boarisk were the lowlifes of the galaxy.

They had no idea what was behind the machine intelligences or what they wanted, only that they had attacked first. Self-defense was a good excuse, but it was only an excuse. The fact was, the ship had been sentient and they'd killed it. He wasn't sure how to deal with that.

"It's firing at the asteroid," Click said as yellow beams of light flashed from the fighter to the asteroid. "*Gold,* you're about to have debris."

"We see it. Shields at max." Connor sounded agitated.

"It's figured out our ploy," Aduncus said. "*Gold,* move now."

But the ship was already swinging out from around the asteroid.

"Guess I can let it go now," Solaria slowly opened her eyes, yawned, and stretched. "That was a bit harder than I expected. But it feels good to stretch the mental muscles."

"Might want to try throwing the asteroid at the fighter," Click suggested. "Might keep it off the *Gold* long enough for them to get a killing shot."

"Good idea." She closed her eyes again and seconds later the asteroid picked up speed, heading toward the fighter.

The *Gold* swooped low as the asteroid went high. The fighter shot the asteroid two more times before turning its guns on the ship closing in on it.

With its first shot, the *Gold* caused the ship's shields to light up a soft blue. Its second shot hit as the enemy ship got off a shot. The *Gold's* beam didn't hit a shield and left a deep mark in the fighter. Then the asteroid hit it. The blue shield reappeared and the asteroid was reduced to rubble, but the shield flashed out and several of the larger chunks got through.

"Thanks, Solaria," Connor called through the coms. "Their shields can take only so much damage before they collapse."

Bright green beams shot from the *Gold*, and when they hit the fighter, it exploded. Shards of metal mixed with chunks of asteroid.

The *Gold* swung around and headed toward them.

"Let's rendezvous with the *Paw*," Connor said. "We need to come up with a plan."

"Definitely," Click replied. "Follow us." He turned the yoke and headed back toward where they'd left Phil's ship with Melody and Leonada.

Skylar looked at the bits of metal mingling with the dust from the asteroid Solaria had bounced off it. For a moment, he could see it as bits of flesh and blood spinning out there in the darkness. If the fighters were as alive as the ship he and Del killed, then they had just ended the lives of three more. They should have been trying to find a way to talk to them, to find out what they wanted. Even if they had attacked first, it didn't feel right to just be trying to wipe them out. If they really were sentient, they didn't have to be evil. They might be able to reason with them.

As they flew away from the latest battlefield, he wondered how he could use Del's new gift to try to stop the fighting and find peace between their species.

10
More Planning

"WOW, WE"VE been following everything on long range scanners," Melody said as Skylar and Solaria returned to *the Paw*. "I don't know who had the better moves, Solaria, Click, or Connor's pilot."

"I didn't realize Solaria had gotten so strong," Leonada said. "Unless Click was helping too."

"He helped with the really big ones we squished the two fighters between," Solaria said, sounding proud of herself. "But the one where the *Gold* was hiding behind it, that was all *me*." She beamed and ran a hand through her long, splotchy platinum and gray hair.

"It was all pretty incredible out there in the middle of it too," Skylar agreed with the girls. "Now, since the *Diver* has slightly more room, Phil wants us all over there so we can get with the Cosmos and try to come up with a plan." Skylar went to the medical kit as Phil had asked him before they left the *Diver*. He needed a couple of things from it which he thought might help Del, since he still hadn't woken up, and Professor Aduncus didn't have the complex med kit on board that Phil had.

"All of us?" Melody ran to the airlock and grabbed her helmet. "I'm glad we're going to work out a plan of attack here. We need to do something. By my calculations, Stars' End isn't going to be able to hold out much more than another day under the current barrage from the ships. They might have some really powerful shields, but each hit is draining their power little by little. Eventually the ships will break through again."

"I don't think Phil's going to handle taking that long to get to Ms. Grissom," Skylar said as he closed the door to the cabinet the med kit had been in. "He's hiding it well, but I can tell he wants to get her out of there."

"Don't blame him," Solaria said coming in from the cockpit with Leonada in tow. "We can only hold off our hunting instinct so long, and when someone we care about is in danger, it's that much harder."

"I think I should stay here," Leonada said softly. "I don't know if I'll have anything to contribute and someone needs to watch the screens."

Solaria took her hand and pulled her toward the airlock. "Look, none of us know what we'll have to contribute, but Phil wants us there. I figure someone from the Cosmos's ship will keep an eye on the screens for us. They've got a full crew, from what I overheard."

Skylar tucked the med kit under his arm as he followed Melody into the airlock. "If the rest of his family is anything like Connor, of course they have a full crew. Corp-brats can't be bothered with doing too much for themselves."

"Hey!" Melody shouted as she got her helmet locked into place. "I'm a corp-brat…, er, kid. For all we know, you're a corp-kid too."

Skylar shook his head. "You're different." Although the money and stuff he'd received from his anonymous father, or father's family, seemed to indicate a powerful corporate connection, he didn't want to think about the possibility of coming from a privileged family.

His mother had worked hard for everything they had. She had complained about the corporations as much as she had the psychics. He'd overcome his fear of psychics, but he didn't want to be forced to see the corporations in a different light. Everything he was finding out about the things they hid from the general populace made them feel even more evil than his mother's ranting about them had. He didn't ever want to feel beholden to a corporation, not for anything.

"Not all corp-kids are the same." Melody moved over to the airlock controls and seemed to be waiting for Leonada to get her helmet in place before cycling the doors. "And not all corps are the same. Some actually help people."

"Your mother runs the biggest personal enhancement corporation in the galaxy," Solaria said, leaning against the wall and frowning toward Leonada who was fumbling with her helmet. "Sure, she helps people look pretty, but there's more to life than that."

"I know, and I wasn't thinking of Glamcor, I was thinking of Intergal Rescue. They are officially a corp." Melody tapped the pad to close the airlock as Leonada got her helmet locked.

"A non-profit corp," Skylar added. "And yes, they do help people. Some of the non-profs help the general populace more than themselves, but as a whole, most corps don't."

The pressure in the airlock stabilized and the outer door opened. They hurried down the ramp and across the asteroid to the *Deep Diver* where the outer door was still open, waiting for them. When they were halfway across the short distance, a ship passed over them and swung around to land on the other side of the *Diver*.

Although he'd seen the *Nubul's Gold* on the viewscreen and sensors, Skylar hadn't realized it was nearly twice the size of either the *Paw* or the *Diver*. The ship's four laser cannons were prominent on the wings above and below, more like a tank than a spacecraft.

"They are a—" Solaria started to say, then shut her mouth and frowned. The emotions rolling off her were an odd mix of anger and frustration.

Skylar realized she'd shut her mouth due to them being on coms and not wanting to piss anyone off by saying something she shouldn't have about the people coming to lend a hand. He hoped the Cosmos didn't have any readers strong enough to hear what she'd intended to say.

Sometimes being in a telepathic society was complex in ways Skylar hadn't thought of until he was part of it. Earlier she'd commented about the Cosmos being paranoid. He wondered if she'd been about to repeat that or something else.

The ship dropped low enough to hide behind the *Diver*. Skylar figured they should go ahead and get on board so they weren't blocking the airlock when Connor's family was ready to come join them. He hurried up the ramp to where the girls were waiting for him.

"You know, sometimes you get so wrapped up in spaceships," Solaria said as she tapped the panel for the door to shut.

"Hey, I never thought I'd leave Hummassa, and now I've got ships all around me. This is great." Skylar almost expected the ribbing he got from her. Out of all their friends, he was the least galaxy-smart one, but he was trying to catch up fast. Since leaving his backwater planet, he was quickly making strides to being well-traveled, and wanted to keep that going for the rest of his life. He didn't know exactly what he was going to be once he graduated from Stars' End, but he wanted to be out in the galaxy seeing as much as he could and not tied to one planet or station for the duration of his life.

"You're a little strange, Skylar," Solaria continued as the airlock cycled and the inner door opened.

Professor Aduncus was there waving them into the ship. "We need to cycle the airlock and open the outer door. The Cosmo family will be here in a moment."

"I'll take the med kit to Phil." Skylar put his helmet and gloves on the shelf and hurried off. He really needed Del to wake up and hoped there was something in the med kit to help with that. After Skylar had woken up fairly quickly after their fight with the machine intelligence, he was worried that Del was still asleep. Professor Aduncus' assurances that it might be tied to Del discovering a new psi talent didn't help, since when Skylar had discovered both his reader skill and his feeler power, he hadn't been rendered asleep for hours. Yeah, with his reader talent, he'd blacked out, but it hadn't been for long. He was worried something was majorly wrong with Del and that somehow, his forcing more power into Del had made things worse than they would've been.

Filzbalm looked up from the back of the couch. He'd opted to stay with Del as opposed to cramming himself into Skylar's helmet again. *"He's trying to wake up. I think he just needs a boost."*

"I hope so," Skylar said as he held out the kit to Phil.

"You hope what?" Phil asked as he took the box.

"Filzbalm says Del is trying to wake up and he thinks he just needs a little something to help him," Skylar relayed. "I hope he's right."

"Filzbalm probably is." Phil opened the box and pulled out a stimpatch. "I'm hoping a bit of chemical stimulation will be all Del needs."

"Hey, you didn't tell me you had stimpatches on the ship," Solaria said as she strolled over to them. "That could've helped me move even bigger asteroids."

Phil frowned at her as he tore open the foil package. "You don't need more stimpatches. I think you've used enough of them."

Solaria huffed. "I'm not addicted to them, if that's what Mom told you. I haven't had any kind of jitters or anything since I used the last one a week ago. I just know they boost my powers and that could've helped."

"Or it might've made things worse." Phil rolled up Del's sleeve and pressed the white patch against his smooth gray skin. "We need to test your new limits. Click is a level nine mover, and you were throwing asteroids around at his level or higher."

A wide grin spread across her face and she flashed her fangs. "Awesome. I might be a level ten. There will be a lot of people bidding for my services when I get out of school."

"We'll see about that in a couple of years." Phil sat in a chair at the table as the distinctive chime of the airlock sounded through the ship. "Now, this shouldn't take too long. If it's going to work, it'll be quick. If not, I might have to try something else." He looked into the med kit that lay on the table. "Yes, I do have a suppressor in here if we need it."

"A suppressor?" Skylar looked at the med kit and didn't recognize anything in it beyond a few bandages and the stimpatches. "What does that suppress?"

"His psychic powers." Phil pulled out a small syringe. "If his powers are what's keeping him asleep, this will help him wake up, although it might retard the development of a new power. He probably has information we need. I know you told us what you felt when you were linked with him, but Del was in direct contact with the intelligence. He'll have different perceptions of it than you had. Right now, we need that information."

Skylar wondered how Del would feel about that. If he was developing the psychic power to communicate with and command machines, or machine intelligences, he might not be very happy if they did something that ended up retarding that ability. Somehow being able to talk to machines sounded like the perfect power for Del. He'd hate not having it to its fullest extent.

As Phil put the suppressor back in the med kit, Del sighed and his eyes opened. "Wow, am I hungry."

"You're awake!" Skylar rushed toward the couch, then stopped as Phil reached it before he did.

"Did we win?" Del muttered.

"You won that fight and we won the one after, but there's still the war to win," Phil said, reaching back to the table and grabbing a cup of water. "Here, drink this and sit up slowly. We've got guests arriving."

Del took the cup in shaking hands and downed it quickly. "Guests? Who."

Footsteps in the corridor from the airlock drew Skylar's attention. He turned as Connor and four other people entered. The older woman had the same tall, lanky look as his roommate and he figured she was his mother. The man who was between them in age, and looked more like Connor, might've been an older brother—Skylar wasn't sure. The other two were also students from Stars' End who had apparently hitched a ride with the Cosmos.

"So, what are we going to do about those strange ships around the academy, and what kind of lock do they have on the stargate?" Connor's mother started without bothering with introductions. "This school is supposed to be home to the strongest psychics in the galaxy. This shouldn't be happening."

Skylar instantly disliked her. He'd gotten used to Connor's occasional bouts of arrogance, but his mother was beyond that. She was expecting everything to be taken care of for her.

"Mother, everyone's on break, or coming back from it," Connor said. "It's just a few teachers and staff in residence currently."

She sighed. "And they couldn't have left stronger people?" She turned as Professor Aduncus walked in. "Professor, surely as the most powerful reader Tursiops has ever produced, you should've been able to stop this situation from escalating."

Professor Aduncus bowed slightly. The move surprised him, until Skylar realized he probably treated most of the parents of his students with respect, and he might have been trying to placate her. "Mrs. Cosmo, I assure you, I have been doing everything possible since my arrival in the system, but we are not dealing with conventional minds here. From what we've been able to learn, these are machine intelligences. We sent you the information we accumulated on your flight this way."

"I glanced at it." She waved away his comment and took a seat at the table. "It sounds preposterous. Machine intelligence? Machines are simply tools. They don't possess the ability to be intelligent."

"No." Del shook his head. "That's not true. Machines are capable of a lot more than we give them credit for. What I encountered on the ship we boarded was a mind, but not one like anyone has ever recorded evidence of before. Its thoughts were very organized and logical. It struggled to deal with us, and for a while, that gave me an edge against it. But it learned from every second our minds were connected. It was powerful. It nearly threw me out." He glanced at Skylar. "If it hadn't been for Skylar and Filzbalm, it would have."

Mrs. Cosmo glanced at Skylar, then appeared to study Filzbalm. "Ah yes, Mr. Mars and the Solar Drake. Most incredible, both of you. I've heard tales, and it seems you're making an even bigger name for yourself."

Skylar wondered what Connor had told his mother about him, and if she was getting information from other sources.

"But this isn't about Skylar," Del said, drawing attention back to him. "This is about the armada blasting Stars' End."

"Del's right." Professor Aduncus seated himself on the couch next to Del. "And now that you're awake, you can tell us more about what you saw and experienced inside the ship we managed to disable."

Disable. Skylar desperately wanted to say they'd killed it, but he held his tongue. From what he was picking up from Connor's mother, she wouldn't be open to the idea that the ships were alive. It was probably a pretty big leap for everyone who hadn't been there in the link with him and Del. Sure, Phil and the professor were going along with it, but he couldn't tell how much of that was real or just placation.

Del glanced at Skylar. "I don't know how much Skylar was able to tell you, but it was incredible. I know I'm not a reader, just a feeler, but I've been in mental links before. I know what it feels like to connect to another's brain, and that's what this was. It was touching the thoughts of another being. The ship is just a—" He made an empty gesture as he struggled to find the right word. "—a body for the consciousness that inhabits it. It's incredible. It's very logical, and I would expect a machine mind to be logical. Computers run on logic, so this would have to as well. But it also knew fear. When Skylar relayed to me some telepathic attack theories, I used those to form my own assault on it. What surprised me the most was the fear that came off it as I struck the fatal blow." He pursed his lips, sighed and closed his eyes. "I might have killed it. I don't know."

"It hasn't done any repairs since we left," Solaria said softly.

Del nodded. "Mistakes happen."

Mrs. Cosmo huffed. "Mistakes? You dealt with a problem. How is that a mistake?"

"No." Del glared at her as anger surged out of him. From the look on her face, she felt it as raw and brutal. "We're taught to never use our powers to harm others. That's what I did. I harmed someone with my talents. It wasn't right."

"Really." Mrs. Cosmo glared at Professor Aduncus. "Aduncus, if this is the effect of the training the students at Stars' End receive, I may have to re-evaluate Connor attending there. We need our children to be strong to survive in the worlds we control. We don't need them weak."

Professor Aduncus straightened and squared his shoulders. "Compassion is not a weakness. We do our best to instill consideration and understanding in our students. Until now, I haven't heard any complaints."

"Look, this doesn't matter right now," Del said, drawing everyone's attention back to him. "If we don't do something soon, there won't be a Stars' End. I don't know why, but the intelligence of the ship was scared of psychics. It sees us—me and movers in particular—as a threat to its existence." He closed his eyes again. "In my case, I think the fear is justified. But one thing I picked up while I was struggling against it, trying to give everyone time to get back to the *Diver*, was that it got a boost from somewhere, like I did from Skylar and Filzbalm. In the moment of that boost, it was like there were several more artificial minds linked to it, and they were pushing it power, the strength to fight me."

"Like a hive mind?" Phil suggested.

"Or networked computers," Melody added.

Del pointed at Melody. "Exactly. Networked. All the ships are networked together."

"Like a bunch of telepaths working as one mind," Professor Aduncus said.

"That would explain the search pattern they set up over Yeldona Three when we were hiding in the atmosphere there." Phil rubbed his face. "This isn't good. It's not like we're going to be able to pick them off one at a time. We've got to deal with their networked minds logically working on the problem of us. I don't doubt they have a bit more computing power than we do."

"I wonder if we'd be able to sever their network somehow." Skylar was slowly forming an idea. "If we could get one isolated, maybe we could study it and find a weakness that we could exploit without killing them."

"They're machines, you can't kill them," Mrs. Cosmo snapped as she hit the table. "We just have to shut them down and then recycle them. Surely that much metal will be welcome in the recycling centers of Ferrous Prime."

Skylar had the urge to ask her if she wanted to be thrown into a compost heap somewhere when she died, but he didn't. He knew Connor wasn't her, but her general arrogance made him realize there might be things Connor hid when he was around the students at Stars' End. Skylar wondered how much Connor brushed off because he didn't want to try to understand things beyond the limited scope his mother had. He knew how hard it had been for himself to change his own thoughts, ideas his mother had pushed onto him for years.

"That might be an option when our conflict here is done," Phil said as calming emotions washed over the room. "But we aren't to that point yet. I like Skylar's thought of trying to separate one from the network. If we could do that, we might be able to reason with it and figure out what can be done."

"You don't reason with machines," Mrs. Cosmo objected. "When they're malfunctioning, you turn them off."

"Can we vote on this?" Skylar asked before they got to the point of out-and-out arguing, which wouldn't do them any good.

Professor Aduncus beamed at him. *"Good idea, Skylar."* "I think Skylar has an excellent idea. Let's take a quick vote. Those in favor of the idea of trying to separate one from the herd, so to speak, raise your hands."

Everyone except Connor, his mother, and brother raised their hands.

"To make this official." Professor Aduncus gestured for hands to go up. "Those opposed."

As expected, Connor, his brother and his mother raised their hands.

"Very good." Professor Aduncus nodded. "Now we need a plan to separate one of them. From what I've seen, our best bet is getting one of the fighters by itself."

"Since they attack in groups, that might be difficult," Click said, speaking for the first time since the Cosmos came on board.

Solaria grinned. "It always makes the hunt more fun when you're trying to pull the weak from the herd."

Skylar leaned against the wall and added ideas from time to time as Solaria, Leonada, and Phil contributed the most to the formulation of a plan to get a fighter by itself. They were approaching it like they would hunting antelopes on the frozen plains of Pantheria.

In the end, Skylar was fairly sure it would work. He just hoped they'd be in time to save Stars' End, and he wondered how many stimpatches they were all going to need to stay awake through the whole thing. It had been hours since any of them had slept more than a few minutes, other than Del, who'd been out for a while. Skylar didn't think that counted for much though, since he'd been healing his mind after the first attack on the artificial intelligence. The name felt right.

11
Finding A Suitable Subject

SLYLAR CLUNG to the asteroid next to Del and Solaria. They had an hour's worth of oxygen in their envirosuits as they waited for the plan to play out. Everything had to be just perfect.

"This isn't a great plan," Del muttered.

"Of course it is," Solaria replied without turning to look at him. "Well, our part of it is. The critical and potential problem is if Click and that guy the Cosmos have flying screw it up. Their pilot might be good, but he works…" Solaria cut off again.

They were being treated as adults and they were all doing their best to act like adults. Skylar knew this and appreciated it, although sometimes he wished he hadn't figured out that being treated like an adult meant not being able to be so open with his opinions, particularly when they needed an idiot's help.

"She's more irritated than she's letting on," Filzbalm said from inside Skylar's helmet. *"She's also very excited."*

"She's hunting, of course she's excited," Skylar replied. He had no doubt that, if Solaria had a tail, it'd be flicking like mad.

"Or if a fighter fires upon them at the wrong moment and hits us by mistake," Del said. "Or any other of a myriad of problems. It could get in a lucky shot on either ship. The shields on the *Diver* aren't top of the line. Any of them could crash into this asteroid. Our thruster packs could malfunction. We could overshoot the ship when we go after it."

Skylar put a hand on Del's arm and projected calming emotions the best he could with Solaria's excitement hitting them both hard. "We're doing the most logical thing possible in this situation. If something happens, we improvise."

"Every hunt is ultimately improvisation," Solaria said. "But don't worry. I'm with you. I'm an awesome huntress."

The *Diver* zipped around an asteroid a couple of space rocks over from them. The *Gold* was right behind it.

"Here they come," Skylar said.

"We're on our way to you now," Phil's voice came over the coms. "We've got six fighters on our tails. You're going to have to be fast. I'd go after the last one."

"I'll see what it looks like." Solaria eased a little closer to the edge of the asteroid. "Bring them in close to us."

"Doing our best," Connor replied. "These guys are majorly pissed off."

The *Diver* passed over them first. The ship was close enough for them to count the rivets in her hull. Then the *Gold* shot past.

One of the fighters behind them fired and its blasts were just meters from hitting the asteroid. The rock they clung to shifted slightly.

"Crap, we didn't take into consideration the pull the ships would have on the asteroid's rotation." Del was tapping something into the pad on his gloves that was linked to his heads-up display in his helmet. "We're going to be out of position."

"Not if I can help it." Solaria's power rippled through the asteroid and it stopped rolling, then reversed its trajectory.

"Okay. Stop now." Del quit tapping on his glove. "If it will, just hold it still."

The first of the fighters zipped by, closer than either of the other ships had been, but hopefully they didn't know Skylar and the others were on the rock, or didn't care.

"Okay, that was closer than we expected," Del said. He started tapping on his glove again. "Two more will pass close enough, but we're going to have to be fast or they'll be out of range quickly."

"That's why we anticipate the speed and trajectory of our prey and move before they pass us by." Solaria's tension was obvious in each word. She sounded like she was about to explode, like a spring wound too tight.

"Then we should move…" Del trailed off for a second.

Skylar got ready to activate his jet pack with the controls in his gloves. He really wished he'd had more than just basic training in their use before setting out, but they didn't have time. They were just thankful that Connor's ship had several on board.

Connor claimed he'd been practicing Z-GBall while on break. Skylar didn't care why they were there—they were important to the plan working. Otherwise, they would've had to send Click instead of Skylar, and Click and Solaria would've had to get Del to the ship using their mover powers. The jet packs left Click flying the *Diver*, which was just as important, and initially more dangerous.

"Now! Go now," Del shouted and took off.

Solaria was half a second behind him.

Skylar hit the control to send himself flying into space. The jetpack felt like it was going to tear itself from his back, even though he had the straps tight. It jerked him into motion, applying several Gs of force against his torso.

"Wings are a lot easier," Filzbalm said.

"Not now," Skylar muttered as he moved his hands the way Connor had shown him to get the desired movements out of the jetpack. He did his best to follow Del and Solaria as the fighter started toward them. He hoped the ship wouldn't notice them until they reached it, and by then, Del would've engaged its artificial intelligence.

Getting the jetpack to travel in the direction he wanted was a lot harder than it had been when they'd done a short flight from the *Diver* to the asteroid. But it was important, and he did his best to stay with them. He wanted it to go faster, but was afraid it would shake him up worse.

Just as he thought he was falling too far behind, an invisible force grabbed hold of him and yanked him forward.

"Don't drop too far back," Solaria said.

Skylar adjusted his flight and felt better up alongside her as they drew closer to the fighter, still in tight formation with the others chasing their ships.

Just as Del reached out for the ship, it fired the gun on the tip of the wing they were closest to. Del yelped and jerked back.

"Del, don't do that!" Solaria shouted, and Del landed on the wing.

"Thanks," Del's breath sounded short and labored. "That startled me."

"No worries." Solaria landed gracefully next to him. "Movers gotta move. Now get to work on this thing. The force of it moving through space is stronger than I anticipated. I'm going to get tired quickly if we don't get inside."

"Working on it," Del said gruffly.

Skylar got his feet on the wing and activated his magnetic soles to help hold him on. The way the space dust and the ship's momentum tore at him, he was thankful he had on the environmental suit. It was worse than the jet pack shooting him through space.

The fighter wobbled, but the hold of Skylar's magnetic soles was enough to keep him from dropping into the dark vastness surrounding them. The weapons on the wing he stood on fired, apparently not targeting their shots, but hitting the fighter flying in front of them.

"Careful with the guns, Del," Solaria shouted through the coms. "We don't need the other fighters turning around and shooting us out of space."

"Trying. It's fighting me." Del's words were short and clipped.

"Filzbalm. Link us all with Del, we've got to help out." Skylar pushed his power out through his connection with the Solar Drake. Again, the crystal shard embedded in his hand grew warm as he felt Del's mind first, then Solaria's. Without words or conscious thought, they added their might to Del's as he battled the fighters. This conflict was different from the way the one with the larger ship had been. The fighter's artificial intelligence was sharper, faster, and wilier than the bigger vessel's. It was used to quickly adapting to a situation.

It went into a roll as if to throw them off.

"Keep your eyes closed, Del," Solaria said.

Del sent energy down into the fighter, trying to gain the upper hand in their mental battle. The ship shielded itself from it. It was like the ship had fought a psychic before. It parried every blow Del sent at it.

"Sever its connection to the herd," Solaria said.

Skylar tried to understand how that would work, then noticed a glowing cord in the mindscape of their battle. It was like a power cable running from the strobing orb-like mass that was the ship's consciousness. He remembered reading about how external connections often appeared like that in the mindscape where psychic battles took place.

"There it is." Skylar pointed and created a mental beam of light to show Del where they needed to strike. He didn't want to risk pulling back enough of his own power to attack the cord.

"Thanks." Del sounded out of breath—even with the extra energy Skylar and Solaria were feeding him. He called up a shield while, at the same time, he cast a bolt of raw energy at the power connection between the fighter and the other sentient ships.

The ship stopped dead in space. Confusion roared up in it. The others had been providing it direction, helping it know its place in the galaxy. Del's attack had severed that connection. It no longer knew what to do.

"Hit it," Solaria shouted.

"I'm not killing it," Del replied. Then he tapped into his feeler gifts and soothed the ship. All feelings of aggression were smothered.

The idea was something Skylar wouldn't have thought of. Del was trying to relax a savage beast, a brain very alien to anything they'd ever dealt with before but it was working. The confusion from the ship ebbed. The ship still floated in the sky like it was dead, but they were all with Del as he maintained a connection to it, keeping it calm.

Then, Del reached into the glowing orb that was the mental representation of the ship in the mindscape. He did something and the orb faded out and became a computer terminal, complete with a touchscreen interface.

"What are you doing?" Solaria looked over his shoulder in both the real world and the mindscape.

"Trying to redo its programming," Del said. "It's really complex."

"You're trying to change the way it thinks? Is that right?" Skylar didn't like to think about redoing the way something thought. When his mother had died, and he'd been found in the forest, his rescuer had been a feeler who had stopped him from grieving and then both Phil and Ms. Grissom had manipulated his emotions. After months of training, he understood why they had done it, but still didn't think that made it right, exactly. But they hadn't been actively trying to rewire the way he thought. That sounded wrong.

"Sometimes drastic measures are called for," Filzbalm said before Del could reply.

There were times the Solar Drake came up with some very profound ideas, and there were times—like this—when Skylar wondered how much of it was Filzbalm and how much of it was the Mother of All Drakes who could telepathically connect with any or all her children at any time.

"Filzbalm's right," Solaria said, having heard him easily since they were all mentally linked. "If this is going to work, we have to declaw it quickly."

Del shook his head. "This isn't going to be quick. I think it will be easier if we go inside and I access the ship's central brain directly. For changes to be long term, I'll need physical access."

"This sounds an awful lot like brain surgery," Skylar said, not feeling up to physically digging through the ship's mind.

"Very similar." Del nodded slowly, then started walking across the wing to the hull of the ship. "This way."

The ship's hull rippled like water where a rock had just been thrown, then an opening slowly appeared in its side. It stopped growing once it was large enough for them to step through. The opening entered onto a short hallway. Once they were inside, it sealed back and was quickly a smooth metal wall.

Remembering the run to get out of the other ship, Skylar couldn't help but wish the hole into space had remained open until they finished what they needed to do and got out of the fighter. He patted his leg, and was thankful he'd once again remembered his multitool.

12
Rewiring

THE INSIDE of the fighter was fairly similar to the larger ship, mostly sleek metal corridors with openings instead of doors. Everything felt more cramped. The first corridor was so tight that Solaria's shoulders nearly brushed both walls as they walked the few feet to the central area Del was looking for. Luckily, the fighter still had light, but for the life of him, Skylar couldn't figure out where it originated. It just was there, as if it was coming out of the metal walls themselves.

For some reason, Skylar was expecting a viewscreen like the other ships he'd been on had, but there was just another metal wall.

"We're near the front of the ship," Solaria said.

"How can you tell?" Skylar was completely turned around after they entered the ship.

"Predator." She smiled, flashing fang for a moment. Somehow it wasn't as threatening behind a helmet as it was when they didn't have a couple inches of clear polysteel between them.

Skylar sighed at her answer to so many questions, even if it was appropriate in most cases.

"She's right," Del said softly, almost dreamily.

Since they had the ship subdued, Skylar and Solaria had turned their attention to other things and dropped back from the link, trusting Filzbalm to let them know if Del needed their mental assistance as he restructured the ship's thinking.

"How are you holding up?" Skylar asked.

"I've never tried this on a human mind, not being a reader and all, but there's lots of little nuances to this." Del frowned at the pillar in the center of the small room. It was a darker metal than the rest of the ship. There wasn't any light coming from it. Like the rest of the ship, it appeared to be of a single sheet of metal. Even where it joined to the metal of the floor and ceiling it was a solid surface, just a slight fading of color indicated any difference in the metal.

"That's what we've all heard," Solaria said. "Your grandfather knows more about the human mind than we do, and he might be better at this, but he's too old for the jet packs."

"But he's still with you," Professor Aduncus' voice filled their minds. *"Now focus on what you need to do."*

It made Skylar wonder why the professor hadn't helped with the initial mental fight to get into the ship. Then he figured if things had gotten too tight, he would've lent his considerable strength to Del.

"Let me see if I can get it to create an interface," Del said.

Seconds later, the metal of the column seemed to liquefy, and formed a touch screen.

"Now this will be easier." Del seemed a little more awake as he began working the touch pad like he'd done with a similar one in the mindscape earlier. He tried several things. Time ticked by and the oxygen levels on their suits dropped.

"Del, we're going to need to get replacement atmogens soon," Skylar said as his oxygen gauge dropped to ten percent.

Del frowned and tapped on the screen. "Let me try something. I might be able to…yes, there is a way…it's going to take a couple of minutes. Sorry I didn't think of this before."

"Think of what?" Skylar asked.

"This ship is airtight. It doesn't have an atmosphere because *it* doesn't need it." He tapped something else on the interface. "But we do. I think it's making us a breathable mix of gases right now."

Solaria pulled out a sensor. "Oxygen levels are rising, along with hydrogen and nitrogen." She frowned. "It's going to be close whether we get enough atmosphere before we run out in the suits."

"Then stop talking and conserve," Del said. "Too bad we don't have anything to filter the air once we manage to make it."

"We have the Paw coming in," Professor Aduncus said. *"We should be alongside in eight minutes."*

"Might not be in time, but just in case, ask Melody to be prepared to come over here. I could use her help with some of the code in this thing." Then Del went silent as he focused on the interface.

"Sit and meditate," Solaria suggested as she lowered herself to the floor. "It'll slow your breathing."

Skylar rolled his eyes as he copied her movement. If there was one thing he was horrible at, it was meditation. It was one of the basic principles of training psychic skills, but he always had trouble with it. There was something about being still that his mind rebelled against. Sure, he could sit and calmly watch the stars go by, but that was a lot different from sitting and trying to get his mind to be still. Professor Aduncus had used a form of ritualized motions to help Skylar learn to quiet his mind, but there were some things being relaxed was good for. Slowing breathing was one thing.

Even though he felt exposed sitting there on the fighter, trying to get his mind to relax and slow his breathing and heart rate, he did his best.

"It's really not that hard," Filzbalm said, barely moving inside Skylar's helmet. *"I do it all the time, when*

there aren't things I need to be commenting on. I'm not sleeping, just relaxed."

"I'm not sure what we'd do if you weren't," Skylar replied with a chuckle, then inward cursed himself for using more oxygen with the short laugh. He told himself that even if they passed out from low oxygen, the professor and Phil would be there soon after. Then he realized that if Del passed out they would most likely lose control of the ship and die.

Del manipulating the ship into creating a breathable atmosphere was going to be their best hope of surviving. When humans were under the influence of a feeler, they recovered from the effects soon after they stopped, either from the feeler ending their sending, or something blocking the feeler. The same was true of readers. He wasn't sure where Del fell on the feeler and reader scale with the artificial intelligences, but he was pretty sure that with as logical as the machine mind was, as soon as Del stopped his manipulation they'd all be in a world of hurt.

"Solaria," Skylar said softly and with as little effort as possible.

"You're not meditating," she said equally as soft.

"Trying to. If either one of us loses our oxygen first, we need to move the atmogens to Del to keep him going until we've got an atmosphere we can breathe, or Professor Aduncus arrives."

She nodded. "Good idea. Now be quiet so we don't have to do it."

Skylar didn't reply. He closed his eyes and breathed as shallowly as he could. He knew the less he breathed, the less oxygen he'd use. He wondered if they'd have had better luck if they'd simply used foot thrusters instead of jet packs and could've used rebreathers instead of atmogens. But then they would've been slower getting off the asteroid and onto the ship. Either way, their plan hadn't been overly perfect.

"No plan ever is," Filzbalm said. *"Now just relax—we're almost there."*

It was always harder to relax when someone told Skylar to relax than if he'd just been sitting around. The oxygen was running out, and he had to be calm until the atmosphere inside the ship reached a breathable level, or until Professor Aduncus and Phil arrived with back up atmogen packs. He closed his eyes and willed himself to stop worrying. Phil had never let him down, neither had Professor Aduncus, and if Del said they'd have atmosphere in time, he'd believe him. He just had to be calm.

Taking a slow shallow breath, Skylar willed his heart to slow. He'd been taught the technique in basic psi-skills class, where he'd been at least two years older than the other kids. He'd struggled with it while the other students mastered it easily. At first, he'd felt like he was always going to be playing catch up to the other kids his age, like Del and Solaria, but luckily, he'd proven to be a fast study in everything but meditation.

Keeping his eyes closed helped. Although there was no way he could forget he was in the strange fighter ship, with his eyes closed, he could imagine something a little different. Something like the beaches back on Hummassa. The water was always warm and relaxing. The three moons there were in similar orbits, so they often rose together, creating a brilliant display on the water. He and his mother used to go down to the beach when she had vacation time and could get away for a few days. They'd camp out and just enjoy life. It was the most relaxed he could ever remember being.

"That's a very pretty place," Filzbalm said, interrupting Skylar's meditation. *"Maybe we can go visit it some time."*

"I'd like that," Skylar replied. He wondered what his good friend Teir would think of Filzbalm. Even months since the attack that had killed his mother and left Skylar an orphan, they still didn't know what had happened to Teir. His body was never recovered and Skylar often wished he had time to go find him, or at least, track down the Boarisk raiders who'd taken him and make them pay. He wasn't free to do that just yet, but he kept track of Boarisk raids across the galaxy and would use that information to find them someday.

"Del says the atmosphere is breathable now, and the Paw just extended its umbilicus over."

Skylar opened his eyes. "Thanks." He undid the magnetic latches on his helmet and lifted it off. The air was fresh and tasted great.

"How are we going to let Phil and the professor in?" Skylar asked as he set his helmet on the floor. "This ship doesn't have an airlock."

"It does now," Del said. "It's incredible what this ship can do. It's like the metal itself is alive. There are some polymers that can take various shapes when an electrical current is applied to them, but it's never worked with metals. I think it will take years to totally discover everything this ship is capable of."

A soft hiss down the corridor they'd come through earlier was followed by footsteps. Moments later, Phil, Professor Aduncus, and Melody appeared in the control room.

"This is incredible," Melody said first. "Did you have to tell it how to create an airlock?"

Del nodded. "Essentially. I think the ship saw a big part of it in my mind and created it accordingly. It's easily as smart as most acknowledged sentients are— more than a lot of them. We've just got to do a bit more reprogramming so it's not trying to kill us."

"Why is it trying to kill us?" Phil asked as he leaned up against the wall.

"I don't know for sure," Del said. "I'm trying to figure that out. I'm hoping if I can get a download of its history we might get a better picture."

"What about its logic circuits?" Melody asked. "That should be at the heart of its basic programming. If we can change its logic then we might be able to get it to stop attacking us."

"Good idea," Del said. "I've got control of it right now, but I'm going to get tired of keeping my mind riding it all the time." A second interface panel appeared in the side of the column. "See what you can figure out. The programming language looks familiar, but I can't put my finger on it."

"It's LISP," Melody said after studying the interface for a moment.

"LISP?" Del sounded confused. "You mean the old human programing code from a thousand years ago?"

Melody started tapping away on the screen in front of her as Del peered harder at his. "See? It's really complex LISP, but it's LISP."

"Wait a minute," Professor Aduncus spoke up. "Does that mean these things come from Sol Three? From Old Earth? How is that possible?"

Skylar stood and started pacing, his mind trying to understand what was happening. "Wait a sec. The other ship, when it scanned us, it declared you guys as hybrids of human and what I'm guessing are…Old Earth mammals, maybe?"

Phil nodded. "That's right."

"So, it knew what both were. Now we get into its code and it's an old human code. As strange as it sounds, the only logical explanation is that these things originated on Sol Three." There were big holes in Skylar's logic, but it felt and sounded right.

"But if that's true, then why don't we have this kind of advanced tech now?" Solaria asked.

"We already know that computer intelligence is outlawed." Professor Aduncus paced alongside Skylar. The simple action made Skylar feel better as he thought through the situation.

"Maybe these ships, or the progenitor of these ships, were from Earth and escaped, or were driven out, when they were outlawed," Skylar proposed.

"And like everything else the corps don't want us to know about, they simply outlawed it, erased it from the history books, essentially making it so nobody ever did it again," Phil added, beaming at Skylar.

"If it happened before we discovered the stargates, that would explain why they're so slow, generally speaking," Solaria said. "They don't have all our tech, but they're more advanced than a lot of the tech we do have."

"Once we discovered the stargates, we spent a great deal of time expanding our minds," Professor Aduncus said as he put his hands behind his back. "We're much more reliant on psi skills than machines for a lot of things. Maybe that was the key to artificial intelligence being outlawed."

"If the psis in charge of the corps couldn't control the machines, they had to go," Phil finished for him and slapped the wall. "Professor, I think that's the key right there, and that's why they see us as a threat. We're psychics. If we weren't, they might have just flown on past Stars' End."

"But that doesn't explain all of this," Skylar said. "The metal, for instance. There's no metal on Earth or any other planet that can do what this metal can."

"Not necessarily." Phil pointed a finger thoughtfully. "We explore planets that may either support human life, or have elements we need. Maybe this metal was something they found on a planet that wouldn't support human life and didn't have an abundance of necessary elements. Maybe it's something they created. We won't know until we find out their history."

"And that's going to take forever," Del said with a heavy sigh. "There's massive amounts of data here, more than we could download externally." He paused and blinked. "Wait a minute, the pressure just backed off." He looked at Melody. "Did you do something?"

"Just erased the human hostility algorithm." She grinned mischievously. "At least, I'm fairly positive that's what that one did. If it's not fighting you anymore, I'm pretty sure I did it right."

"How did you know what to delete? I was trying to make sense of the code and it was gibberish," Del said, staring at the console.

"I've spent years studying old coding languages. Call it a hobby." Melody continued to grin. "I'm not a really strong feeler, and figured I never will be, so I decided to do smart girl things."

Del nodded and chuckled. "I totally understand."

"Wouldn't it have been easier to run it through a translator?" Skylar asked.

"I doubt a modern translator would've caught much," Melody said. "It's the computer equivalent of those hieroglyphics you found on Pantheria, just a little newer over all. There's a lot of code that doesn't make sense to me. We'll have to study it over time and figure out exactly what it does."

"But if you've managed to get the algorithm removed in this one, how hard will it be to do the same thing with the other ships?" Phil asked.

"If we had several people with the new gift Del's showing, it might work over time, but right now, we'd have to get both of us to each ship and disable that code from their main control system. It's not practical," Melody said.

"How susceptible is LISP to viruses?" Solaria asked.

Melody shook her head. "I know the language, but I don't think I could come up with a virus to interact with their run-time environments, not to mention getting it to them. At least, not quickly, that is."

Del sighed. "If the same trap worked twice, we could get another fighter, and it would take a couple of us to subdue it without breaking the network link. But if we could access it like we are this one, we could deliver a virus to the network, unless the others realize what we're doing and find a way to block it."

"If they're as smart as it appears they are, I doubt we can use the same tactics twice and hope to win," Professor Aduncus said. He swung his arms a bit, a behavior Skylar recognized from their training sessions showing he was thinking. "We just proved they're reluctant to chase us into the asteroid field in small numbers, and they're quicker to fire on us than they had been. When we stop and look at their behavior, they had surrounded Stars' End and seemed to be studying the academy until we *killed* the one vessel."

Their coms beeped.

"Grandfather, we've still got two on our tails." Click sounded frantic. "We're coming back your way. Have you got good news?"

Del shook his head. "We can't try again so soon. Melody and I still have work to do here." Then his face brightened. "But I might be able to help. Click, head right toward us. We'll take care of the fighters."

"What are you going to do?" Skylar asked as he continued to pace. He wished they had more time and could try the same trick again, or something close to the exact stunt.

"Well." Del heaved a heavy sigh. "I hate to try to do this, but we're going to shoot them out of the sky."

Skylar's stomach knotted. "Is that right to do? I mean, you'll be forcing a sentient ship to kill others of its own kind."

"Under normal circumstances, it would be an abuse of power," Phil agreed. "But these are not normal circumstances." He glanced at Professor Aduncus who nodded. "Del, if you can manage it, get this ship to shoot at the others. Maybe it will be easier if you could disable—"

"No." Aduncus said solemnly. "If we just disable their weapons or propulsion and they're still connected to the network, then we'll still be in trouble. They'll be able to report back everything we do." He shook he head and pinched the bridge of his nose. "I know this is harsh, but we're fighting for our survival here. Del, if you fire, you're going to have to shoot to kill."

With pursed lips, Del nodded. "I understand." He closed his eyes.

After a second, Skylar felt the increasingly familiar tingle of Del's power brushing his own. He wasn't sure, and didn't even know if anyone else in the galaxy would be since Del's mental ability to communicate with the artificial intelligences was totally new, but he felt really strong. Professor Aduncus-level reader strong.

The ship vibrated. The metal floor flowed under their feet.

Skylar wished he could levitate off it. "What's happening?"

Solaria rose several feet in the air. "What do I hit?"

"Don't worry," Del said.

The floor rippled and several spikes of metal rose up, then flattened out on the tips. After a couple of seconds they took on the look of chairs.

"Make yourselves comfortable." Del tapped a couple of things on his console. "Melody, while I see about getting control of the weapons, see if you can create a viewscreen. I understand why the fighter doesn't need one, but I think it would be nice."

"I do too, but I think we'd need to give it the atomic formula for clear polysteel and I'd need to look that one up," Melody said.

"Oh, good point. That might have been something humans came up with after they left Sol Three, and they wouldn't know about it." Del dropped into a dream-like speech pattern. Skylar wondered if he was in deep communications with the ship and was having trouble doing that and talking at the same time.

"Yeah, I got nothing," Melody said. "I'll keep digging, but until then, I think I can make us a screen on the central column so we can keep track of what's going on outside." She tapped a couple of times and then a panel like the ones she and Del were working on appeared. It had a graphic display of the solar system similar to the one Skylar had been watching earlier on Phil's ship, but it looked a lot more complex, like the ship's sensors were vastly better than the ones on the *Paw*. Each asteroid near them was perfectly rendered. Some of them were different colors, or had streaks of color. The mass representing Yeldona Three was a multitude of colors and textures. The ships attacking Stars' End were several different shapes whereas on the *Paw*, they were all just dots.

"Interesting," Phil said, looking over Skylar's shoulder as Skylar took the seat closest to the panel. "Del, are you providing the advanced scan here, or is that normal?"

"Normal, from what I can tell." Del still sounded dreamy.

The ship shuddered again.

"Good shooting," Click said through the coms. "You brought down the two ships we'd missed. Nice clean shots."

On the viewscreen, the two ships closest to them went from bright orange to gray silhouettes of the fighters. A lump rose in Skylar's throat. They had killed again, and worse this time, they'd gotten the ship to kill two of its own. There had to be a word for that kind of murder, but he couldn't think of it.

"We're trying to survive," Filzbalm said. *"We keep hearing how harsh the galaxy can be—well, we're getting to see it firsthand."*

"I know, but that doesn't make this any easier." Skylar wished he could shut the Solar Drake out for a little while. At least while he dealt with the feelings running through him. He didn't want any of the others to know what he was feeling. From what he could sense, Del was having the same misgivings he was about killing the machine intelligences, but he doubted Solaria would understand. She was a predator, after all.

"Let's rendezvous with the others and see what we can come up with for the next step in our plan," Phil said. He looked at his wrist and the embedded screen of his com. "Stars' End only has a couple more hours before her shields give out. We need to figure out how to get in there and retrieve our people."

"En route to the asteroid as soon as you get back to the *Paw* and disconnect the umbilical," Del said. "Who's staying and who's going?"

"I'll go with Uncle Phil," Solaria said.

"Staying with the fighter," Melody said. "There is way too much new info here."

Del chuckled softly. "I don't think anything could pry me away from here for a while."

Skylar wanted to stay with Del and be there in case his powers were needed. On the *Paw*, he'd just be an extra person. "Staying, if that's okay."

Phil nodded. "Fine with me. Solaria, let's go join Leonada. We'll see everyone else on the asteroid. Professor, I presume you're staying with Del."

Professor Aduncus nodded and crossed his arms. "I'm staying with my grandson."

Having Professor Aduncus with them made Skylar feel a little better about being on the strange ship with no way to get off if something went wrong. There were too many variables they hadn't taken into consideration. He just knew that at any moment, any number of things could go horribly sideways, and he wasn't ready for that. He was tired and wished they could get everything wrapped up so they could all get some much-needed rest after their break from school.

13
Slipping Behind Enemy Lines

"DOES SHE have a name?" Leonada asked as they flew away from the asteroid after they'd had their latest discussion and made a new plan.

"Does who have a name?" Skylar tried to figure out what she was going on about.

"This ship," Leonada said from her seat near the wall. The ship had added more seats to accommodate the people riding in it toward the armada assaulting Stars' End. "All ships have names. This one needs one, or should have one. How about it, Melody? Del? Who does it think of itself as?"

"That's silly, Leonada," Solaria said. "We don't think of ourselves by our names, they're just the names our parents gave us."

"Filzbalm told me his name," Skylar said, remembering when he'd finally gotten the dampening bracelet off when he was near the Solar Drake and Filzbalm had announced who he was. "Maybe the ships think of themselves by names…or numbers."

Del shook his head. "Not from what I've been able to tell."

"Maybe that can be something we can program into it," Melody said. "I'm still working on some of the physical recordings while Del's working on the mental stuff. It really is a unique combination of mind and machine."

"Not that unique," Solaria said. "There's a whole armada of them out there."

"But Leonada has a point, and Del, you and Melody might want to start working that into what you're doing," Professor Aduncus advised. "By giving the ship a name, an identity, we might make it easier for it to adapt to not being part of the network. Make it truly unique."

A slow smile crept across Del's face. "And if we can convince it that we've freed it from the network that had been controlling it, maybe we can be more like friends, and I won't feel like a puppet master here."

"I'll start working on that from my end," Melody said.

"And I'll do what I can as we get closer," Del said.

Skylar wiped his hands on his legs, even though he still had his gloves on and the action just smeared the sweat on the inside of them, making him feel strange and a little icky. They were flying toward the armada. The other ships were going to slip into the atmosphere of Yeldona Three and hopefully hide there while they tried to make it to the school, rescue people and get back out.

There was a lot that could go wrong. They had no idea how the armada was going to react to one of their ships that wasn't part of the network anymore, or what would happen if the armada tried to force the ship back into their shared link.

"Any idea what we want to call the ship?" Melody asked after a couple of minutes.

"Mighty Huntress," Solaria suggested.

Skylar rolled his eyes and was thankful she couldn't see him, 'cause she would've snapped at him.

"Sleek Shadow," Leonada added.

"Why are you making the names sound female?" Skylar asked.

"'Cause it's a ship?" Solaria didn't add "silly" to her comment, but it was there in her tone. "All ships have female names."

"Tell that to the Cosmos who named their ship *The Nubul's Gold,*" Skylar said, trying to find a good argument against giving a fighter ship a girl's name.

"They're humans, corporate humans no less," Solaria said sharply.

"What about *Rescue Paw One*, or *The Deep Diver*? Those aren't specifically female names," Skylar continued. The discussion was helping him take his mind off the mission they were on and letting him relax, at least a little bit.

"We're not naming *our* ship anything like *Rescue Paw One*. I love you, Uncle Phil, but that's a very unoriginal name," Solaria continued to argue.

"Our ship?" Skylar asked. They hadn't discussed ownership of the ship—besides, it was an intelligent ship. Ownership sounded like slavery, and they weren't the Boarisk. He didn't want a slave. But he did like the idea that they had a ship of their own, or at least that they could make friends with. A ship who might take them where they wanted to go.

"Sure, salvage law says that whoever finds wreckage owns it." Solaria tapped the arm of her chair. "With everything, Del and Melody have done to get the ship to not kill us, we could argue that we had to salvage it, and that makes it ours."

"But if we're going to view the ship as its own sentient entity, then will it be right to claim ownership?" Professor Aduncus joined into the discussion.

"The government might complicate that a bit," Phil said. "Remember, artificial intelligences are illegal. If we succeed in what we're doing, both in saving Stars' End and getting this ship reprogramed, we might not want to advertise to the galaxy that she's a living ship…or at least, not a thinking one. The debate of life is going to be a lot more complex. We might be best off altering its outer appearance and doing as Solaria suggested by claiming salvage. We can take a couple of stargate jumps to create a data trail. And if we do everything right, nobody will be the wiser."

Skylar liked the sound of the plan. It was feasible. If they survived the next couple of hours, it just might work.

"It shouldn't be that hard to alter its appearance," Del said. "From what I've been able to determine, nearly every part of this ship is adjustable, malleable—" He shrugged. "—I don't know what else to call its strange fluid metal. But it looks like it can become nearly anything we need it to, within its mass limits. It has a limited amount of metal that can only be stretched so thin."

"Could it consume one of the destroyed ships for additional mass?" Solaria asked.

Skylar's mind recoiled at the idea. "That's disgusting." He turned in his seat and stared at her. "Really disgusting."

"Why?" She looked confused. "The other ships are just floating out in the asteroid field, useless. If it needs additional mass, why not absorb it from them? One of them shed mass—split into two—like an amoeba, and some creatures eat the skins they shed."

"But they aren't eating the bodies of their dead," Skylar said. "That's just not right."

"Other than agreeing with Skylar on it sounding somewhat cannibalistic," Del said from his seat at the column, "I think it might work, so we might be able to feed it scrap metal to increase its mass. Once we get out of this, we'll have to think about the ethics of that."

"I think this is enough conversation for the moment," Melody said. "We're nearing the first of the larger ships. We don't know if their sensors will pick up us talking or not. If we have to speak, telepathically might be the better option."

"Linking us now." Professor Aduncus was suddenly in Skylar's head. Even with his training, the professor was strong enough to slip into his head without notice, but their practicing together might have had something to do with that.

"Thanks, Grandfather, but let's keep it quiet," Del said. The mental presence of the ship still loomed large around him. *"I'm working really hard to make this operation run smoothly."*

They all went silent.

It was long and nerve-wracking, sitting there in the ship and not being able to talk. The only way Skylar knew where they were amongst the armada was the display on the column that showed them slipping past the first of the large ships, heading toward Stars' End.

The ship they passed wasn't one of the ones firing on the station. From what they'd been able to tell from their distance observations, the ships were rotating their assault. Several would move close to Stars' End and fire for a while, then fall back and others would take their place. The smaller fighter ships were doing the same thing. The only thing they could figure was the ships needed time to recharge from their attacks, but even after taking control of the fighter they were flying in, they still hadn't figured out exactly how the ships were powered.

According to the screen, they had passed the second line of large ships, and were fast approaching the line firing at the academy.

"Thirty minutes until the station's shields are drained," Phil said through the link.

The reminder didn't help Skylar's stress levels. Once they linked with the station, they would have to move quickly. If Ms. Grissom and the others weren't ready to run, they weren't going to get everyone in time. He just hoped they had room for everyone.

The cows in the farm area entered Skylar's mind. During his time working the farm, he'd grown to like the cows. He was worried they wouldn't have enough space for the people and the cows—in fact he was fairly sure they didn't have the space. He didn't want to leave the cows behind, but people came before cows.

"They're going to need to drop their shields for us to get in," Del said. *"Grandfather, can you reach Ms. Grissom and ask her to drop long enough for us to get through?"*

"Hope none of their fighters rush in with us," Solaria added.

Del stiffened.

The mindscape became crowded. Something was reaching out for their ship.

"They're trying to reestablish the link to their network," Del shouted. *"They're really strong. We're literally in the middle of them and they're hitting us from all sides."*

Although Professor Aduncus was providing the center for their telepathic connection, Skylar and Filzbalm poured strength into Del as fast as they could. *"Draw from us, shield, block them out."*

Power lashed out of Del, and in the mindscape, the attacking ships were pushed back.

On the physical plane, Del was panting in his seat at the column. Skylar knew this was a lot more psychic power than Del was used to controlling. He was used to being a level two feeler, and the smartest kid in school. This was way beyond that. Even after handling the crystal claw, Skylar wasn't sure he'd be up to being the focus of what Del was enduring.

"We're with you, Del," Professor Aduncus said. *"Think of something concrete, something strong. Make your shield out of that."*

For a moment, it felt like Professor Aduncus was going to become the focus for Del, but he didn't. Like all of them, he lent his considerable strength to Del. The shard of the crystal claw in Skylar's hand burned with the power that was swirling around them.

Almost reflexively, Skylar gathered up all the power and focused it through the crystal and then into Del, so the external strength he received was one unified source and not seven. The act made Skylar feel stronger—then more power joined them. Ms. Grissom and the other teachers were helping.

Skylar hadn't known so many minds could work together. They empowered Del. The raw force of all of it burned Skylar's hand. He glanced at it with his normal eyesight and was surprised to see that his glove wasn't ablaze. In the mindscape, his whole hand was glowing bright gold as he gathered everyone's power and fed it to Del, who used it to shape a massive shield around himself and the ship, blocking the other artificial minds from reaching it and bringing it back into their network.

"We're at the station's shields!" Melody shouted.

"Coming down," Ms. Grissom replied. *"Be quick."*

Something rocked the ship.

Del screamed. The ship screamed. They nearly lost the mindscape battle. The shield started to fall.

"Del, fight it!" Skylar hollered as he yanked power from everyone and drove it home to Del.

His shield held, but he was bent over his knees shaking. *"We were hit. A physical attack with the psychic. I don't know if we can withstand another one."*

Behind them, the station's shield went back up, but glowed with the absorbed energy from the repeated attacks of the armada.

Skylar gasped for breath—he hadn't realized how hard it was keeping an energy flow going, even with the help of the other minds.

"We've got backup on Stars' End," Professor Aduncus said aloud. "If the other machine intelligences are firing on us, we have to assume they've figured out they aren't getting this ship back."

"We hope they aren't," Skylar said, still wishing they had a viewscreen or port that they could use to see more than just computer-generated representations of things.

"I think while we're getting everyone on board, we should get what weapons we can," Solaria said.

"They aren't going to do us a lot of good against ships," Skylar said. He was getting tired of disagreeing with her. It was something he wasn't used to doing. They were normally on the same page with everything. In the midst of everything going on, he wished they could go back to easily working together.

"Maybe not, but if we need to, we can stand on the wings of this one and shoot them as they shoot us," she snapped. "I don't want to go down without a fight."

"And we won't," Phil said. "Right now, we're fighting the best way we can, psychically."

"Stargate just opened," Ms. Grissom said through their link. *"Ships are coming through, but I can't make out ID yet."*

"We'll be docked in thirty seconds," Melody said. "We can worry about the ships later."

"Right. At thirty minutes, they might not reach the station in time," Phil said as he got out of his chair. "Del, see if you can make more room in the back for people."

Del sighed as he straightened in his chair. "I'll try. The shield seems to be holding for the moment. It helps that the ship is assisting and not fighting me."

Skylar glanced at Professor Aduncus. "Should I stay here with Del, or do you need help getting people on board?" He didn't want to move. He wanted to stay there and keep feeding power to Del, but he was also growing desperately hungry and doubted Del had figured out how to create a food dispenser, let along program it.

"Stay with Del," the professor said. "I'll bring you both back some food and drinks. I think we could all use something." He followed Phil out.

Solaria, Melody, and Leonada stayed with Skylar, and they watched over Del.

"This is starting to feel normal," Solaria said softly.

Skylar turned and looked at her. Her eyes were partially closed and she was breathing slowly. "What's starting to feel normal?"

"Linking our minds like this. You're doing something like what Aunt Blizza and you did with the claw back on Pantheria, aren't you?" She didn't open her eyes.

"I'm not sure. I think so." Skylar looked at his hand, which had stopped burning but was still warm. "The crystal did something that makes it easier for me to do this, to link people and channel their power."

"I don't care where it's coming from, I'm just thankful it's working," Del said with a heavy sigh. "I couldn't do this by myself. We'd have lost the ship back to the network by now."

"Wow, those are some huge ships coming through the stargate," Melody said, causing Skylar to look at the screen in front of him.

There were three ships through at that point and looked like at least one more coming. They were easily half the size of the large AI ships. From what the sensor said, they were armed to the teeth and loaded full of life forms. It was scary how much data they had at their disposal.

Skylar passed his hand over the screen and a line appeared between the incoming ships and the station. They were twenty-five minutes out. He wasn't sure how long it would take them to get within weapon's range and what the armada's response would be, but under the current barrage, the station only had twenty minutes left. If they were coming to rescue the station, they were going to be five minutes too late.

14
Caught In The Blast

"WE"RE GOING to have to shoot our way out of this, aren't we?" Skylar said as the first people from Stars' End entered the ship. From his estimate, they had about fourteen minutes before the station's shield collapsed.

Solaria nodded. "We'll be the prey when we leave the station."

"We should head toward the rescue ships that are coming in," Filzbalm said. *"They might be close enough that if we get a fast start we could make it to them before we take too much damage."*

As he relayed the Solar Drake's idea, Skylar looked at the screen. A dozen heavy war ships cleared the stargate and were headed toward the school. He was impressed, and wondered who had managed to get that many ships ready to go in a short period of time.

"It makes sense," Solaria said. "Prey always runs to the herd for protection. We would only have a short period of time when we'd be vulnerable."

"Unless the rescue ships start shooting at us," Leonada said. "We are in one of the enemy fighters."

Skyler sighed. "Good point." Then an idea hit. "Hey, Del, anyway you can get the outside of this thing to look like either *Rescue Paw One* or *Deep Diver*?"

"I don't know if I can pull that off, but I can probably get it to not look so much like one of the fighters." Del tapped his interface.

"The fighters are currently attacking the rescue ships," Melody announced. "They're swarming the incoming ships. Looks like the cavalry brought fighters of their own."

"Most likely Ruby Guard," Ms. Grissom said from behind them.

Everyone turned and stared at her.

"Ms. Grissom," Solaria said first. "Uncle Phil was worried about you."

"And I've been worried about all of you." Ms. Grissom walked over to where she could see the panels they were all watching. "You kids were supposed to be on school break, not off having all kinds of misadventures. You're lucky you survived as long as you have."

"Got our fingers crossed to keep surviving," Del said. "I'm trying to get the exterior of the ship to change so the rescuers don't shoot us down. I don't have as much mass to work with as I'd like, but luckily Astara is helping me as much as she can."

"Who's Astara?" Everyone asked at once. The name rang out in the metal room, and somehow sounded like it belonged there.

"Well, we were talking about getting a name for the ship and I asked her what she would like to be called," Del explained as he continued working at his station. "She had to think about it for a while. She's not used to the idea that individuals have names as designations. She is used to being called fighter Twelve Thousand Eighty-Five. But she came up with it. I think it sounds good."

"See, I told you ships were female," Solaria said smugly.

Skylar rolled his eyes. "And you couldn't have explained this to us a few minutes ago?"

"We've been busy." Del lifted his hands from the interface. "That's about as much as we can change the exterior without her absorbing some of the mass from the station, but that would cause structural damage and we don't want that."

"That might not matter in a few minutes," Ms. Grissom said sadly. "We have no idea how much damage those ships will do when our shields finally fail."

"We've got to do what we can to save the school," Skylar said. In the past months the school had become his home—he couldn't imagine losing it. He'd already lost the home he'd shared with his mother on Hummassa, and he wasn't ready to lose the school too.

"We are," Ms. Grissom said. "You all have rescued us. A school is much more than just the structure that houses it. It's the people, the staff and students, that make up the heart of a school, and as long as you all survive, so will Stars' End."

"I've got a com signal to the incoming ships," Melody said. "Astara's coms are a bit old by our standards, so I had to show her how to reconfigure things to get the best signal out. I've got Admiral Temer on the connection."

"Can you put it on speaker?" Ms. Grissom asked. "Unless you can link with our coms?"

Melody shook her head while she tapped away. "Too complex at the moment. We've got lots of changes to make to Astara to integrate her tech with ours. She's a marvel, but we've made advances since the AIs left Earth." Melody paused. "Okay, Admiral Temer, I've got Ms. Grissom for you."

"Ms. Grissom?" A deep male voice came through the connection. "Where is Principal Fuspatula?"

"Mr. Fuspatula was on break when the attack started and hasn't returned. He's due back tomorrow," Ms. Grissom replied. "In his absence, I'm in charge of Stars' End."

"Very well," he continued. "I'm Admiral Temer of the Ruby Guard, on dispatch from the president to resolve your problem. Our sensors indicate your shields are on the brink of failing."

"Seven minutes," Skylar said, looking up from his screen to Ms. Grissom.

"That's correct, Admiral." Ms. Grissom flashed Skylar a quick smile. "We're in the process of evacuating the station. We should have everyone on board our experimental spacecraft in about two more minutes."

"My people tell me we'll be to you in ten, and within firing range of the larger ships within five. What can you tell us about the species that is attacking you? At this point they're resisting our scans. Their fighters are like nothing we've ever fought."

"That's because they're machine intelligences," Ms. Grissom replied.

"Ms. Grissom, you do realize that machines don't possess intelligence?" He sounded like he didn't believe her. Skylar understood because at first none of them had believed it either. "Could these simply be pre-programmed drones, and there's a mothership hiding in the system somewhere?"

"If you can find the mothership, I'd like to know about it. The fighters and the larger ships are all part of a network of intelligent machines."

Phil rushed into the main chamber. "We're all loaded. Del, have the ship seal itself back up."

"Astara, disconnect from Stars' End," Del said. "Stay within the station's shields but fly around so we can exit as close to the rescue ships as possible."

"Shield failure in thirty seconds," Melody announced.

"We should have more time than that." Skylar leaned closer to his screen, wishing the room wasn't getting so crowded and he could actually move around. They weren't going to have time to get away. If the ships or their fighters managed to get off a lucky shot and take out the school's reactor, they could all be destroyed before they got to safety.

"Looks like the deterioration has become exponential." Del gripped the edges of his chair. "Everyone hold on, leaving as fast as we can."

Astara lurched hard.

Skylar grabbed hold of his seat like Del had, but his back and neck still hurt from the acceleration. Ms. Grissom went tumbling forward, as did Phil. They ended up in a pile. From the shouting from down the corridor, the people in the back of the ship had been caught off guard. Then Astara rolled.

"They're shooting at us," Del shouted. "We're trying to evade here."

Not taking his eyes off his screen, Skylar watched as they headed toward two of the larger AI ships that were still firing on the station. Four fighters were following them. Del and Astara were shooting back. One went spinning off and crashed into Stars' End, its small orange dot vanishing into the large green cylinder that represented the station.

Then the station vanished from the screen.

"Hold on!" Melody screamed. "Concussion wave!"

Something hit Astara and she went tumbling end over end in space.

Skylar tried to hold onto his seat, but he couldn't. On the second flip, he flew out of the seat and smashed into the central column. He tried to get a hold there, but the smooth metal was too slick for him to get a purchase. As Astara spun out of control, Skylar bounced off the floor and made a mad grab at the shafts the seats were mounted on. They were small enough for him to get his hands around and at least stopped him from flying all around the cabin.

"Filzbalm, are you okay?" Skylar reached through his link with the Solar Drake.

"On your leg. I'm fine. Help Del keep the mental shield up to block the network. If that fails-"

"I've got Del protected physically," Solaria said through the active group link. "Let's keep him and Astara going."

As he clung to a shaft, Skylar poured power into Del. The network had continued to struggle to get Astara back. Even as they fought everything around them, the network didn't let up.

They stopped rolling through space.

"I didn't do that," Del said. "Astara didn't do that."

"Tractor beam!" Melody shouted. "One of the big ships has us in a tractor beam."

Skylar got himself back into his seat. He stared at the screen as they were drawn toward the huge ship. He barely saw it. His gaze focused on the spot on the screen where Stars' End had been minutes before. Tiny bits of wreckage showed up on the screen where his latest home had been. His throat tightened and tears ran down his cheeks.

He hadn't been allowed to properly mourn his mother, Teir, or Hummassa, but everyone was too busy to stop him from crying about the loss of his dorm room, and the cows that hadn't been able to be rescued. He wondered when the galaxy was going to stop taking things from him. The cows, like his mother, hadn't done anything to deserve their fate. They had just wanted to live their lives in peace, and that was torn away from them—torn away from *him*. It wasn't right.

As they moved steadily toward the huge ship, he wondered how much more the thinking ships were going to take from him and his friends. He hit the screen and poured every ounce of power he could through the link and into Del. It was the only way he could think to fight back. He had to keep them all safe.

The crystal shard in his hand blazed with power. It seared through him. Skylar screamed and then realized everyone else on the ship was screaming with him. Power lashed out at the ship pulling them in. It hit the network and everything went black.

15
Captured

EVEN THOUGH he couldn't see out, and the screen in front of him was flickering, Skylar could tell they were still moving forward. It wasn't a lot of movement, but either the tractor beam continued to pull them, or their general momentum was carrying them toward the larger ship.

Skylar rubbed his head, wishing his headache would go away. "Del, what's happening?" He'd thrust out so much power. He was wobbly, but knew they had to keep going.

"Wow. Skylar, that was one hell of a blast." Del sounded tired. The rest of the ship was eerily quiet. "I think you knocked out their network."

"And everyone around us," Filzbalm added, landing on Skylar's shoulder.

Skylar glanced around the main room of the ship at the people scattered on the floor. They weren't trying to get up, but here and there some of them groaned softly, or shifted like they were asleep. His drawing power and hitting the ships with it had drained everyone to the point of knocking most of them out.

"Skylar, don't do that again, please," Melody mumbled from the console next to Del.

"Melody, how are you still up when it looked like I took everyone else out, drained them?" Skylar wanted to check everyone, but he needed to know from Del what was happening.

"I guess I was in the link at the same point Del was, so you didn't drain as much from me as everyone else. I don't know for sure." Melody tapped her screen.

"From what I can tell, we've disrupted the network, but the ships are still active." Del swiped and tapped at screens. "Astara says the ships are weak, but still a threat. But the fleet has arrived."

"So, the tractor beam still has us?" Skylar's screen stabilized and displayed the fleet firing on ships and them still approaching one of the larger ones. The smaller fighters were heading for the fleet and the larger ships were moving away from where they'd been firing on Stars' End and heading to engage the Ruby Guard. The only one of the larger ships not moving was the one they were heading toward.

"Yes," Del replied. "The beam is weaker, but still holding us. Astara has tried to reverse out of it, but to no avail. We're about to try firing on the ship to disable the beam. The only good thing is, with the network down, the ships have stopped trying to force her back in and I can divert more of my attention to getting things done other than fighting them off."

"Good." Skylar wanted to be able to do more too. Since they were stable, he slipped out of his chair and went to Solaria. She was breathing, and seemed like she was asleep. Next to her, Ms. Grissom was in the same state.

He'd never dreamed he could draw so much psychic energy out of people that he could render them unconscious. He just hoped there wouldn't be any lasting effects on any of them.

"They should all be fine, once they wake up and have something to eat," Filzbalm said. *"Think of how you feel when you overexert your mind."*

Skylar rubbed his head again. He didn't need to think about how he felt—he was there. The only thing keeping him on his feet at that point was his determination that they were going to get out of the situation they were in. He desperately wanted to make sure everyone was safe. They had to get away from the artificial intelligence ships and to safety.

Astara shook.

"Fire volley," Del announced. He frowned. "Doesn't look like it did any good. The ship's shields are still up and strong. Okay. Astara says they aren't at full strength, and if we keep firing, we could probably break through."

"Then I vote we keep firing," Skylar said. "Or will that drain our power?" He paused and realized there was so much more they didn't know about the AI armada. "What is her power source anyway?"

"It's really complicated," Del said as he worked his screen. "We don't have time or spare brain power to go into it right now. But yes, if we continue to hammer away at the ship's shields, it will drain our reserves, which are already low after providing a breathable atmosphere and rearranging the interior of the ship to make room for the people we rescued."

Skylar straightened from Ms. Grissom and walked over to Del. "What if we wait until we're inside the ship's shields to fire again? Would that work?"

Del closed his eyes, and Skylar got the distinct impression he was communicating with Astara. He wondered if he looked like that when he was talking with Filzbalm. Solaria said he had a tell that let her know when he was doing it, but she was a predator and picked up on things like that a lot easier than most people would.

"Okay." Dell opened his eyes. "Astara said that might work, but the tractor beam controls are far enough inside the flight deck that to score a direct hit and take them out, would also blow the ship. If we're inside its shields when it blows, she's not sure she'd survive."

Skylar sighed. "Then that's out. What if we can disable the tractor beam and then make our escape?"

"You mean send people onto the ship and destroy it from there?" Del said. He didn't close his eyes, but did get a slightly glazed looked. "That would work. The ship would fight us every step of the way. We would have to be quick."

"We need our movers awake." Skylar said. "Do you know if anyone brought a medkit with them?"

"What are you looking for?" Del asked as he pulled up a different screen. This one looked like an outline of Astara.

"Stimpatches," Skylar said, leaning over Del's shoulder for a better look at the screen. "How's yours holding out, by the way?"

"Decent. I think I've got another hour or so. I wonder if I got through your power thrust easier because of it." He began inputting data into the screen.

"Maybe."

"Yep, somebody thought to bring some. Can't tell how many."

"Who?" Skylar stepped away from the column.

"Not sure. But I can direct you there. Head back into the hold."

"Hold?" Skylar paused and stared at Del, trying to understand what he was talking about.

"That's what I'm calling the expanded back room. Like a cargo hold." He shrugged. "Doesn't it make sense?"

Skylar nodded and resumed walking. "Yeah, it makes sense."

The slight corridor between the control room and the hold was littered with people. It made for a major obstacle course as Skylar didn't want to step on anyone, but a few times he had to since there were too many folks piled on top of each other. He really hoped no one was smothering anyone else. But everyone he looked at appeared to be breathing, just asleep. He hadn't gotten a good feel for the number of minds he'd drawn power from—he'd just pulled everything they'd offered.

The farther into the mass of sleeping people he went, the worse he felt about what he'd done to them, but he'd needed to do it. He'd needed every erg of power he could get from them to break the connection with the network. It had worked, but he was still worried some of them might be suffering from what he'd done.

"Head to the back," Del said through the coms as Skylar finally reached the hold.

Astara shook. The sensation was momentary, but nearly knocked Skylar off his feet. Filzbalm help on to Skylar's shoulder tight enough, his talons pricked through the leather patch on Skylar's shirt.

"What just happened?" Skylar asked as he continued to try his best not to step on people, and if he had to, not to step on anything he knew was delicate.

"We're inside the ship's shields," Del replied. "About three minutes until we reach the ship."

Skylar stared across the room full of sleeping bodies. He didn't have time to continue cautiously stepping around, or over each one, but he didn't want to run over them either. He wished he was a mover and could levitate himself across them.

"Filzbalm," Skylar said as an idea hit him. "Del, your sensors up there can detect Filzbalm, right?"

"Sure." Del chuckled. "I've had to explain to Astara who and what Filzbalm is, but she can detect him."

"Good. Filzbalm, fly over to where we need to go. Del, tell me through the coms where he needs to fly."

"Smart." Filzbalm shot off Skylar's shoulder and flew across the hold in the direction they'd been heading.

"Wow, we should've thought of that a few minutes ago." Del paused. "Tell him to slow down—he's moving almost faster than Astara can track. Okay. He's nearly there. Four people to his left."

"Four people to your left," Skylar said.

"He's right above the stimpatches," Del said.

"You hear that, Filzbalm?" Skylar peered across the people, trying to determine who Filzbalm was hovering over. There were a lot of the teachers and staff Skylar hadn't met since he didn't have any classes with them. There were also students in the group, kids who hadn't gone home for the break. If Skylar hadn't gone to Pantheria with Solaria, he would've been one of the ones left behind at the school.

"The person below me, a Mustaphian male, appears to have a shoulder bag that is lying on top of him." Filzbalm landed on someone Skylar couldn't make out.

"Can you get into the shoulder bag?" Skylar thought about using their link, but every time Filzbalm spoke to him, it drove spikes of pain through his brain, and he wasn't sure he wanted to feel what it would be like to send thoughts to Filzbalm. He just hoped the acoustics in the room were good enough Filzbalm understood him.

"I think so." Filzbalm seemed to be tugging at something. After a moment he appeared to make some progress, then he vanished from view.

Afraid someone had rolled over in their sleep and possibly pinned the Solar Drake, Skylar almost started running across people to get to him before he said, *"I'm in. I think I've found them. At least, they look like the ones Solaria used in the tunnels on Pantheria."*

"Sounds like the right thing. Can you fly them here?" Skylar asked.

"Not all at once, but I think I can carry two at a time," Filzbalm appeared in the same spot he'd disappeared from moments before.

"How many are there?" Skylar hoped there were enough to wake everyone up, but knew that was unlikely.

"Six." Filzbalm launched himself into the air and laboriously carried two of the small foil packets across to Skylar.

"So how many?" Del asked through the coms. "I'm dying of curiosity up here, and we're just seconds from being in the ship."

"Six," Skylar relayed as he took the first two from Filzbalm and the Solar Drake headed back to get more. "That's not many."

"It's not," Del agreed. "We need to start with Grandfather and Ms. Grissom. They aren't movers, but they are two of the more powerful people on board. They can tell us who else to wake up."

"Solaria too," Skylar said as he watched Filzbalm reach his destination and once again disappear into the pouch. He wanted Solaria awake. He needed her advice on what they should do. Her predatory instincts didn't often lead them wrong.

"Okay. I wonder if any of the mover teachers are back there," Del said. "Movers would be useful and the first ship was afraid of them."

"Right." Skylar nodded, but he didn't know any of the mover teachers. Ms. Grissom and Solaria would though. "I'm going to head back. Filzbalm can keep bringing me patches. If we're going to be in the ship soon, we need people awake."

"Exactly," Del said as Astara shook again. "We're in. Skylar, you need to hurry."

Doing his best to move quickly, Skylar jumped and hopped around people in the hallway to get back to the control room. Filzbalm reached him with two more patches as he cleared the doorway.

Skylar ripped open the two packets and knelt between Ms. Grissom and Solaria. He put the first one on their counselor's neck—it seemed better than slapping it on her forehead. Then he reached for Solaria and paused.

"Remember, on her palm," Del said. "Her fur slows down the absorption."

"Right." Skylar had been trying to recall where Solaria had put the patches the last time she used them. There had been so much happening then, it was hard to keep all the details of everything straight.

Ms. Grissom took a deep breath as Skylar stood and walked over to Professor Aduncus. While he ripped the package open for the patch he was about to apply to the professor, Solaria jerked up.

"Hey, somebody gave me a stimpatch." She grinned and stared at her hand. "Put it in the right place and everything." She glanced around as Skylar straightened from putting the patch on the professor. "Skylar, you're my new favorite person."

Ms. Grissom sighed. "Why are you putting stimpatches on us?"

"We're still in trouble and we need people awake," Del said before Skylar could. "We've just been tractor beamed into one of the large ships. The Ruby Guard are here and blasting ships and fighters, but we need to get out of this one."

"Okay." Ms. Grissom stood and looked a little wobbly despite the stimulants running through her system. "Bring me up to date."

"No time," Skylar said. "We need movers awake, and besides Solaria and Leonada, I don't know who any of the others are." He wished Click was with them and not on *the Deep Diver*, wherever it was at that moment.

"Movers." Ms. Grissom nodded, then rubbed her forehead like she still had a bit of a headache. "That makes sense. Readers and feelers won't be of any use against these machine intelligences. Professor Ruff made it on board—he's a level ten mover. Professor Malacanty is here—she's a level eight—and Ms. Calibry, from the kitchen, is a level five."

"That's all the stimpatches we've got," Skylar said as Filzbalm came back with the last two.

"Where did you get the stimpatches?" Ms. Grissom asked taking one from Skylar and looking at the package.

"There's a Mustaphian man in the back with them," Skylar said.

Ms. Grissom frowned. "A Mustaphian man? Professor Glicken? What was he doing with them?"

"Don't know and don't care right now," Skylar said, starting toward the hall. "We need to apply these to people and get them awake before the ship we just entered forces its way in and starts killing people." He didn't know for sure that what was going to happen, but he felt pretty sure, based on how the other ship had acted, that was a likely series of events. With any luck, they'd be faster than the ship who was probably a bit disoriented from being cut off from the network and hopefully a little slow on the uptake.

"Right." Ms. Grissom started after him. "Let's find everyone and make a plan."

Skylar was tired of plans—so far, they had only been marginally successful, and he hoped she wouldn't make things overly complex. They didn't need complex—they needed quick and easy so they could turn off the tractor beam, get back to Astara and get free before the Ruby Guard blew up the ship they were in and them along with it.

16
In The Line Of Fire

EVEN THOUGH Ms. Grissom had wanted him to stay on board Astara and help her start waking the others, Skylar explained to her that the movers needed someone to act as a go-between for them and Del, who would be directing them where to go from Astara. He could also help watch out for danger since he and Solaria had more experience with the AIs than the movers they'd woken up.

They found several plasma rifles on the combat instructor, Professor 'clOrdie'ce, an Octogian with six arms. Skylar wished they'd been able to wake him and take him with them, but they didn't have any more stimpatches, and the professor resisted Ms. Grissom's mental probe to wake him.

Skylar held one of the plasma rifles, Solaria had another, and Ms. Calibry had one. The others were going to rely solely on their mover ability.

As soon as Astara opened a door for them and extended a ramp, the fighting started. Professor Ruff gestured and the five tentacled cylinders, identical to the ones Skylar had found on the other ship, went flying across the landing bay to smash into the far wall. They looked rather mangled and didn't rise. Two of the more humanoid models approached. Professor Malacanty dispatched them, but they didn't hit the wall as hard. Solaria fired twice and melted them into slag.

Solaria grinned. "I want one of these, and I need to take more of Professor 'clOrdie'ce's classes. Combat and hunting are very similar."

Skylar didn't bother telling her none of them had any idea if there would ever be classes again. Stars' End was gone. Blown to smithereens. He had no idea what was going to happen to him. At least Solaria, Del, and Melody had families they could go home to. He didn't have anything, but he tried not to dwell on that as he followed Professor Ruff across the landing bay.

"Del, we've got two corridors—which one do we go down?" Skylar asked through the coms.

"Right one," Del replied. "The left one goes to a storage area and won't be of any use."

"Right corridor," Skylar passed along to the others.

As they approached it, the opening started growing smaller.

"I think it's on to us." Solaria sprinted toward the opening.

"This isn't good," Skylar said.

"I've got it." Professor Ruff reached the door and stopped with his arms and legs spread. Power radiated out from him. The metal trying to seal them off stretched across his telekinetic shield as if it was trying to find the edges.

"Move it!" Professor Malacanty slithered between his legs and out the other side.

Solaria jumped, diving past him and rolling down the corridor.

Skylar and Ms. Calibry reached Professor Ruff and slipped between him and the wall as the metal reached the edge of his shield and started around it.

"Keep running," Skylar urged as they cleared the door. "It'll be collapsing the corridor around us next." Being inside a living starship that was capable of reconfiguring its insides was going to make their job that much harder.

"Astara and I are going to try to distract the ship," Del announced. "I hope it'll be enough to give you guys some breathing room."

"I hope so," Solaria replied without breaking stride. "Not sure how much we're up to after Skylar knocked us out. Even the stimpatches are only going to do us so much good."

She gestured and slammed several of the smaller cylinders into the walls hard enough to shatter them. The ship was definitely fighting back and they needed all the help they could get.

They rounded a corner and a line of the humanoid constructs stood there. They looked like they were determined to not let the party pass.

Skylar wished he'd had time to ask Astara if these things were independent AIs, or if they were some kind of extension of the ships. Not that it made a whole lot of difference—they were standing between them and their goal. If they were going to get the ship free, they had to go through them.

Professor Malacanty waved her short arms at them. Two in the middle went down.

Ms. Calibry fired her plasma rifle as she huffed to get her breath. The helmet of her envirosuit was so fogged, Skylar was amazed she could see out of it. She managed to hit one of the constructs, slagging its torso. Its legs and head collapsed to the floor. "This is a lot harder than preparing meals for you lot."

"Just keep firing," Solaria said as she took one out.

Skylar fired too. His shot wasn't as good as Ms. Calibry's. He clipped the thing and it spun twice before going down.

"Aim for the center of the body," Filzbalm said from Skylar's neck.

"Trying," Skylar muttered back. *"If you think you can fire this thing, come out and help."* His next shot took off the thing's head.

"Left at the next intersection," Del said. "We're distracting the ship's main system, but I think it's trying to use auxiliary controls. The bots seem to be similar to a biological person's antibodies."

"So, you've stopped it from closing off its corridors on us," Solaria said. "But it's possible that the more we attack its internal systems, the more it'll fight back."

"Possibly," Del said. "Trying to get Astara to understand the concept and she's struggling with it."

"Don't worry about that right now," Skylar said as he and Solaria took out the final construct with two shots that struck at the same time, sending it sailing backwards. "Just keep this thing off balance so it doesn't close us in these corridors." They took the next one at a jog, then slid to a stop as four huge constructs faced them, each armed with large guns that were aimed their way.

"Get down," Professor Ruff shouted as he gestured and created a shield between them and the energy bolts coming their way. The bolts hit his shield and blazed bright in the corridor.

Professor Ruff took three steps back and exhaled hard. "Don't know if I can handle many more of those."

"Then we switch out," Solaria said. "Let me get up a shield, then you drop yours."

"Better idea," Skylar said. "While you switch out, let Ms. Calibry and me get off some shots."

"Good idea." Ruff sounded exhausted. "Ready."

Skylar aimed his rifle and glanced at Ms. Calibry, who did too. "Yes."

"Now," Ruff said and staggered against the wall.

Since these weren't humanoid, Skylar wasn't sure where they should shoot—he just aimed for the center of the boxy body where the end of the weapon was and fired. Apparently, Ms. Calibry aimed at the same spot on the same bot. They struck hard and forced it back down the corridor with a smoking hole in its weapon. Seconds later, it exploded.

"Great shots," Solaria said.

"But there's three more of them." Professor Malacanty stated the obvious. "I don't know if we have enough strength to take them all out."

"Won't know until we try," Skylar said. He wasn't sure he liked the professor's fatalist attitude. They had to try. If they didn't try, they might as well go back to Astara and wait for the ship to either tear into them or the Ruby Guard to blast them out of space.

A barrage of fire hit Solaria's shield. She sagged slightly. "Wow, those things pack a punch. Professor Malacanty, you get ready for your turn. Skylar, Ms. Calibry, aim."

Skylar nodded. "Okay."

"Fire." Solaria said as she dropped her shield.

Skylar hit a different one than Ms. Calibry did that time. They both damaged the bots they hit, but didn't have the same explosive results as when they'd hit the same one.

"We need to hit the same one next time," Skylar said as Professor Malacanty raised her shield.

"Sounds like a good idea," Ms. Calibry replied.

They waited, but another volley didn't come from the bots.

After almost a minute, Solaria looked at Skylar. "I think they're on to us."

"They might be," Del said on the coms. "But if you let me or Grandfather coordinate either through the coms or telepathically, we might be able to take them by surprise."

"Let Professor Aduncus handle it," Professor Ruff said as he sighed and straightened from where he'd been leaning against the wall. "You should keep your concentration on this vessel and keeping our ship free of its influence."

"Good idea." Del cut his com connection.

"Are we all here?" Professor Aduncus asked.

There was a mental round of confirmation.

"Ruff, you sound a little weak. Are you sure you're ready to take over from Malacanty?" Professor Aduncus asked.

"I'll be fine," Professor Ruff replied. *"The stimpatch is helping me get my energy back a lot faster."*

"Yeah, these things are great," Solaria added.

"Okay. Malacanty, get ready to drop your shield. Mr. Mars and Ms. Calibry, prepare to fire." It felt good having Professor Aduncus coordinating them.

Skylar relaxed. *"Ms. Calibry, let's hit the one on the right."*

"Good."

"Drop and fire," Aduncus said.

Skylar and Ms. Calibry fired at the same time as Professor Malacanty dropped her shield. Their beams lashed out and hit the bot on the right. Its weapon exploded after it rolled back in the corridor, almost exactly like the first one they'd hit together had.

Two beams of force came hurling down the corridor at them.

Professor Ruff shoved his hands forward and his power rolled out. The beams struck it, mere inches in front of Skylar and his party. Professor Ruff shook his head, but his shield held.

"A little easier with just two of them shooting now," he muttered.

"Then let's make it even easier," Skylar said. *"Solaria, you ready?"*

"Let's do this." She sounded excited by the battle, and Skylar had to remind himself about her earlier

comment about combat being similar to hunting. She seemed more bloodthirsty than normal, and he wondered if it wasn't a side effect of too many patches in the recent weeks.

"Which one?" Ms. Calibry asked

Skylar felt odd being the one making the decision with so many adults and teachers in the mix, but he didn't mind. *"Let's go right again."*

"Then we're ready?" Professor Aduncus asked. When they all replied yes, he said, *"Drop and fire."*

Professor Ruff dropped his shield and Skylar and Ms. Calibry fired. Like before they hit and the bot exploded. But the bot was faster and managed to get a shot off before it went up in a pillar of flame and sparks. The other one also got off a shot. Like Skylar and Ms. Calibry, they had focused their fire. They, or the ship controlling them, were learning quickly. Their beams flew down the corridor as Solaria expanded her shield out. It was just a matter of thoughts, but the beams got through before their shield filled the corridor. It hit Ms. Calibry.

She screamed as she glowed for a second. Her body thrashed as if she were struck by lightning. Then she was reduced to a pile of ash. A sickening smell of burnt meat filled the hallway.

Skylar stared. He'd never seen anything like that before. It was horrifying.

"No!" Professor Ruff shouted. He struck out at the remaining bot. Since his attack was mental instead of physical, he didn't need Solaria to drop her shield for him to get through. His telekinetic blast roared down the corridor glowing with a force like raw fire. Professor Malacanty added her force to his and they shattered the bot from the inside. Its metal parts exploded, sending bits and pieces in all directions. Some of them pinged off Solaria's shield, and Skylar was thankful it was there as he dropped his rifle and ran to where the lunch lady had fallen.

There was nothing remaining of her but ash. The bot's beams had broiled her in an instant, and there hadn't been anything they could've done. Ms. Calibry had always had a big smile for everyone who came through the lunch line. Before they'd woken her up on Astara, he'd never spoken to her beyond telling her what he wanted to eat, but he would never get to talk to her again. The AIs were taking so much, and they were going to have to fight hard to stop them.

Solaria touched Skylar's shoulder. "We need to keep moving. We'll mourn her and the others when we're done."

Skylar straightened from where he'd knelt and then stopped himself from touching the pile of ash. It seemed wrong to disturb her further. Picking up his rifle, he nodded. "Yeah. We need to get out of here."

"Hall is clear," Professor Ruff said, sounding gruff and angry.

"Del says you're almost to the tractor beam control," Professor Aduncus said quietly.

"Then let's get it turned off and get off this death trap," Professor Malacanty hissed.

As Skylar followed the others on down the corridor, he realized that if the AIs had always lashed out at the biological people, he could understand why they'd been outlawed. It hadn't been for the reasons the corporations told everyone, but it had been for a good reason nonetheless. They were dangerous, and he hoped Melody and Del were right and had managed to remove Astara's hostile algorithms. It would be a really bad thing if they ended up fighting Astara again, particularly if something happened to Del.

As they turned the corner, Skylar glanced back at the pile of ash. It was the only thing still in the corridor.

The bot parts were already being reabsorbed by the ship. The AIs didn't even mourn their dead, they simply reused their parts. It was cold and very logical. Skylar wanted to end the fight and never have to endure it again.

17
Shoot And Run

TWO MORE turns and they'd reached the tractor beam controls. Skylar wondered why they weren't closer to the docking bay, or all the way in the central control column, if the ship was designed the way Astara was. There was a small room that had controls for several things that he didn't have the foggiest idea how to identify. The smooth panels didn't seem to have any kind of interface or switch to turn them on. A few of them appeared to be add-ons—they either stuck out of the wall or hadn't been completely integrated into the metal, but even those didn't have any buttons or switches that were detectable.

"Del, what do we break?" Skylar asked through the coms.

"You're going to have to do a lot of damage to it so the ship can't repair it quickly or easily," Del replied. "There should be a panel with a graphic interface."

"Ah, Del, why would a machine intelligence need a graphic interface for something like a tractor beam?" Solaria asked as Skylar noticed a couple of interface panels and tried to figure out which one they needed to break.

"Some of the systems, like the tractor beam and some weapons, aren't completely integrated into the ship's main systems," Del replied. "Think of them as add-ons. Astara doesn't have a tractor beam because they haven't replicated enough of them for the fighters to get them yet. Apparently, the more complex the tech, the harder it is for them to get it right."

"So this is also old tech," Solaria said with a wicked grin.

"That's right. Although the basic idea of tractor beams hasn't changed in hundreds of years, this one is one of the earlier designs," Del confirmed.

"Good." Solaria glanced at Skylar and the two professors with them. "If nobody has a better idea, stand back. I'm taking this tech down."

"What are you thinking?" Professor Ruff asked with a raised eyebrow.

Solaria lifted her plasma rifle. "These things do a ton of damage. Del said break it good. This will do that."

"She makes an excellent point," Filzbalm said.

"Sounds good to me." Skylar hurried back to the entry of the room and lifted his gun.

"Sometimes the easiest application of force is the best," Professor Malacanty agreed as she rushed out of the room.

"Whenever you want to shoot," Professor Ruff said from behind Professor Malacanty in the hall.

Skylar tried to remember actually seeing the mover instructor move, then wondered if he'd teleported out to make everything faster. As he adjusted the plasma rifle from short blast to continual stream, he glanced at Solaria. "Ready when you are."

"Let's blow this place to hell." She hit the panel for the tractor beam first, and as Skylar's beams joined hers, they laid waste to the rest of the control room. Long slashes of melted slag decorated the shiny metal walls. The melted bits dripped down to the floor. Within seconds, the place looked like people had gone mad with laser torches in there.

As Skylar released the rifle's trigger, the wall was already flowing as the ship started repairing the damage.

"We need to get back to Astara—it's not going to take this thing long to put itself back together. Del, we've taken out the tractor beam and anything else that was controlled from this room, but it's already repairing."

"We're doing our best to distract it," Del said. "Better get back here fast."

Professor Ruff took off down the hall back the way they'd come with everyone else following close behind him. Skylar ran alongside Solaria with Professor Malacanty bringing up the rear.

They didn't encounter any problems until they reached the last hall, just feet from where they should've found the landing bay. The hall ended in a solid wall. Skylar skidded to a stop with the others.

"Now what?" Skylar said. "I guess we can try to burn through the wall."

"Let's step back and see what we can do." Solaria moved back to the last bend in the corridor. The professors and Skylar followed her. "Continuous beams again." She raised her rifle and gestured for Skylar to do the same. He wondered if it would've been more effective if they still had Ms. Cailbry and her rifle in the assault.

He and Solaria fired together. He was a little off in his targeting and struck a few inches below her, but they were soon hitting the same spot and using the rifles like laser welders to cut through the metal. About halfway through, Skylar's rifle sputtered and died.

"What?" He stared at the rifle, then turned it over. The indicator in the handle that showed the power levels was empty.

Solaria's beam ended too.

"I don't think we're getting back that way," Professor Ruff said. "We need to find another way."

"Del, we can't get back the way we came," Skylar said, hoping Del was listening to his com.

"Del's almost overwhelmed right now," Professor Aduncus replied. *"Let me see if Melody can get you the information you need to return to us."*

Skylar's heart pounded hard. He didn't like the idea of Del being overwhelmed when he wasn't there to help bring everyone together and provide him with more power. Although Professor Aduncus or Ms. Grissom could help him, there was something about the crystal in his hand that made it easier to merge minds together. Skylar desperately wanted to help Del, but first, they had to find a way to get back to Astara.

"Instead of going left as you did the first time, go right," Professor Aduncus instructed. *"With any luck, Del will keep the ship off you."*

"What's happening?" Skylar asked as they rounded the corner. He wished there was an atmosphere and he could've sent Filzbalm on ahead, but the Solar Drake was stuck in his helmet until they reached Astara.

"The ship we are in has managed to reestablish a link to one of the other ships. They are trying to repair the network that connects them together. Del and Astara are trying to stop them, but their mechanical minds are almost too fast for them. We're doing what we can to aid him, but he's the only one with the gift to communicate and control the machines." Aduncus sounded stressed through their mental connection.

They came to another intersection.

"Professor, which way do we go?" Skylar asked as he skidded to a stop.

"Melody says go through this intersection, then take the next right," Professor Aduncus advised.

Skylar and the others followed his directions. Again, it struck Skylar that he was taking the lead with professors following him, or were they just following Professor Aduncus? It didn't really matter as long as they all got back to Astara and got off the ship.

The whole ship shuddered.

"What just happened?" Skylar asked as they rounded the right turn Professor Aduncus had told them to make.

The ship shook again.

"The rescue fleet is firing on this ship," Professor Aduncus replied. *"Melody needs to try to make contact with them as Del continues to fight the ship and the others it has joined with. She says to make two more right turns and you'll be in the landing bay. Hurry, everyone— we need to get out of here."*

Skylar didn't pause, nor did any of the others as they rushed down the corridors that all looked the same. If it hadn't been for Melody's directions, he was sure they would've been totally lost within a few turns.

They rounded the final intersection and spotted Astara sitting in the landing bay. The walls around them rippled and started to close in.

"Faster!" Skylar shouted and ran for everything he was worth.

He shot past Professor Ruff, who'd actually been in the lead for the past two turns. Skylar knew he was the only one without the mover gift. The others might be able to hold off the walls if they turned completely against them. If he was out of the way, they wouldn't have to worry about him.

He was nearly to the landing bay when the floor turned liquid. He missed a step and stumbled. The metal tried to close around him as he pulled his foot up to keep running. "Guys, it's trying something different."

Professor Ruff grabbed Skylar under the arms. "Go still."

Skylar was hefted into the air. He stared down and realized the professor was levitating both of them a couple feet off the floor that was trying to consume them.

Professor Malacanty flew past them, flying straight out, looking like an arrow as she passed them. Solaria was a round black ball as she shot past them. It reminded Skylar of a maneuver she'd pulled one time while practicing for Z-Gball. She'd curled up and propelled herself across the playing field. Afterwards she'd said something about it being easier to propel herself using her mover skills like that. She was more aerodynamic as a ball than as a humanoid.

As the floor and walls reached for them, they moved quickly down the last few feet of the corridor and into the docking bay.

"We're coming in!" Skylar shouted as they got closer, hoping the professor could relay it to Del and the airlock would open. He didn't want to be trapped inside a ship that was trying to absorb them into its structure.

As Professor Malacanty reached Astara, the airlock opened and she flew in, finally landing. She leaned up against the wall, panting as Solaria, Professor Ruff, and Skylar joined her. The way Astara's airlock closed was just like the way the structure of the other ship had attacked them, and for a moment, Skylar was worried the other ship was using the same technique to go after Astara and try to bring her back into the network.

Then air filled the small room and the other door opened so they could get back into the hold. Skylar let out the breath he'd been holding and rushed inside.

There were still people lying on the floor, but more of them seemed to be awake. Phil was kneeling next to someone a few feet away from the airlock.

"You made it back. I think they could use some help in the main control room." Phil pointed down the short hall toward the chamber where the column was.

Skylar didn't need to be told twice; without a word, he took off running. Del needed him, and he was there and could help. He just hoped there were enough people awake who could lend their power to get them out and to safety.

Everyone who'd been in the corridor and the column room were on their feet. Skylar pushed past them. A few of them he recognized from school, but he didn't stop. He had to get to Del.

In the main control room, Del slumped in his chair with his hands on Astara's interface. Professor Aduncus and Ms. Grissom stood on either side of him with their hands on his shoulders and their eyes closed. It was obvious they were giving him what power they could.

Skylar slid in between them, put his hand on Del's back, and slid his mind into the link they'd already formed.

Del was exhausted. Even in the mindscape, he was barely standing. Around him the presence of Astara was strong. The ship had almost recreated itself. It was firing against two dark presences that kept lashing at it. With each strike, the brilliant glow that was Astara dimmed slightly.

"Give Del and Astara your power," Filzbalm urged. *"Our power. We have to make her strong enough to fend them off."*

Skylar didn't need to be told twice. As tired as he was, he poured everything he had left into Del. Filzbalm did too. Then Skylar felt the crystal in his hand and reached out to the psychics on the ship, the ones who were awake and those still sleeping off the effects of the last time he'd drawn their power out of them. The raw energy blazed through him and into Del. After a second, Del straightened and Astara brightened.

Her beam outshone the attack from the other ships. She pushed them back.

Astara shook violently.

"We're leaving," Del said.

Astara's attack on the other ships intensified. For every beam they shot at her, for every tentacle of dark power that lashed at her, her light shot three beams at them. They recoiled.

The next shake from Astara, Skylar recognized, were her guns firing in the physical world. She was having to blast out of the landing bay. He may have been able to disable the tractor beam, but they were still prisoners unless Astara could shatter the landing bay doors.

He wished he could see what was going on in real life, but he just kept pouring power into Del.

"Stop!" Phil's voice rang through the mental landscape. *"Skylar, stop. You're drawing too much from some of these people. You're killing them."*

"No!" Skylar instantly broke contact with Del. He dropped the connections to all the other psychics on Astara. He wouldn't be responsible for killing people. He hadn't known it was possible to drain people to the point they died. He wanted to curl up into a ball and cry. He hadn't meant to hurt people; he'd just been trying to save them.

Solaria hugged him. "It's okay, Skylar. Everyone's going to be okay. Phil stopped you in time. We're going to be fine."

"We're clear of the ship," Melody said. "I've got a connection to Admiral Temer. He says we've got safe passage from the Ruby Guard if we can get away from the AI ships. He's going to try to give us cover."

Astara lurched and Skylar knew she was flying as fast as she could to get them out of the battle zone. Around him, people moaned and rubbed their heads as they slumped in their chairs or on the floor.

Although Skylar couldn't see what was happening around them, Melody was at her post and stared at the screen, bleary eyed.

"Over half of the AIs have been taken out. The rest are making a run for the stargate," Melody announced.

"Why are they running for the stargate? They won't fit," Skylar said as he lowered himself down to the floor with his back to the central column. He was so tired he just wanted to sleep for days. He wished they had a few more stimpatches to get him through the next few hours until everything was wrapped up.

"The big ships look like they're trying to undergo mitosis like that first one did," Melody said. "If they split in half, they'll be able to fit."

"And if they have access to the stargate network we're going to be in huge trouble." Skylar forced himself to stand. "Get ahold of Admiral Temer. I bet if he can hit the ships at the point of splitting, he might be able to do more damage."

"Good idea," Professor Aduncus said. "The other ship was weaker where it had divided. Maybe their shield will also be weaker at that point as well."

"Relaying that," Melody said.

"Astara agrees," Del whispered. He sounded like he could barely stay in his seat. "They don't normally reproduce like this unless they are somewhere they are safe. They are weak when they divide, but they are desperate to incorporate the stargate technology into their own."

"That's what the virus AI in the stargate had been doing," Melody said hitting the column. "It's been trying to figure out how to incorporate the stargate tech into the AIs."

"We can't allow that," Professor Aduncus said.

"Can we stop it without blowing the stargate up?" Skylar asked, trying to get his tired mind to think of some way to prevent the AIs from having access to the whole galaxy and being able to carry their war with psychics on to a much larger theater.

"Only if we can stop the ships," Del said. "And we'll still have to deal with the AI that's invaded the gate."

"Relaying all this to Admiral Temer," Melody said. "Would it be easier to just put him on speaker?"

"Sure," Ms. Grissom said. "He's our military might in this fight."

Skylar used the central column to support his weight. He couldn't believe they were talking about blowing up the stargate. That would cut off the Yeldona system from the rest of the galaxy until they got a crew out to rebuild it. But without the stargate, it would take years for a crew to get to them to fix it. That would also mean years until Stars' End was rebuilt. It wasn't right that one hostile group could cause that much damage to things. They had to find a way to stop the AIs before it came to blowing up the stargate.

18
Cracking

THE RIDE away from the ship was rough. Even without the Ruby Guard firing on them, Astara still had to dodge shots from the other AI ships. By the time they cleared the firefight, Skylar wasn't sure what made him more nauseous—nearly killing people by trying to get enough power for Del and Astara to win the fight, or the ever-shifting ride. He understood that desperate times called for desperate measures, but he'd been acting without thinking everything through.

He stared at his hand even though he couldn't see his flesh under the envirosuit's glove. He half expected the crystal to have grown out of his hand and be visible in the black polyskin that covered him, but it hadn't. His hand looked like it had before. He didn't know what he was going to do. He couldn't go around just stealing people's power and their lives no matter what the cause.

"We'll learn to control it." Filzbalm rubbed his head along Skylar's jaw. *"It was a mistake. Anyone can make mistakes."*

"But this mistake almost cost people's lives." Skylar kept his back against the central column and his head on his knees. Every so often he had to grab hold of the center post of the chair in front of him, but he didn't feel like he had the strength to sit in it.

"We didn't kill anyone," Filzbalm started.

"Only because Phil stopped me." Skylar was hoping no one was listening in on their conversation. Most

everyone was trying desperately to keep their seats, either in chairs or on the floor.

"Phil is a good man, and a good teacher, even if he isn't a real teacher like at the school," Filzbalm said. *"He understands what we are all going through. I'm sure Professor Aduncus understands too. They all do."*

"Filzbalm, I don't know if I could've lived with myself if someone had died." Skylar shook his head and did his best not to cry or throw up. *"We've lost so much. The school is gone. I don't want to hurt people. If I hurt people, then I end up turning into the person my mother always feared psychics to be."* His mother had been deathly afraid of psychics his whole life. Finding out he was a psychic had been hard for him to deal with until he made friends, saw positive examples of psychics, and bonded with Filzbalm. But if he became what had terrified his mother her whole life, he didn't want to live with that. He *couldn't* live with that. He'd be better off putting a dampening bracelet on and going back to Hummassa, where the natives didn't often have psi skills. However, then he'd have to leave Del, Solaria, Melody, and his other friends behind. With the school destroyed, would they all be together anyway, or would they go their separate ways—or, at least, the ways their parents wanted? And where did that leave Skylar?

"We're clear," Melody announced, making Skylar glance up toward her and Del.

Del was still slumped in his seat with his hands on the interface in front of him. His hands moved across the interface almost too fast to follow. Skylar wondered what he was doing, but was afraid to stand and look, scared someone might read the anguish on his face, or that his nearly empty stomach would revolt and make a mess in the control room. He doubted Astara had bathroom facilities. Most likely AIs didn't need them, and the fighter hadn't been designed for passengers, let alone their comfort.

"Come to the flight deck on *The Vermillion*," Admiral Temer said over the com system. "You can regroup there. If you would like, inform your other ships to meet you there."

"We can do that, Admiral," Ms. Grissom replied, releasing her grip on her chair as Astara's flight leveled out.

"We're making good time finishing off those larger ships as they try to divide," the admiral continued. "But they seem to be learning and trying to block us from attacking the ones dividing."

"They are intelligent," Ms. Grissom said. "We've been trying to tell you that."

"These are starships, not people, Ms. Grissom. There has to be something on them that is controlling them."

Ms. Grissom closed her eyes and rubbed the bridge of her nose. "Admiral, my people and I have now been on two of these ships, and there are no life forms on them."

"We'll treat these things like the drones they are and then see what we can do about finding a carrier signal back to the people who are controlling them so we can stop them before they attack us again."

For several seconds, Ms. Grissom was silent. "Very well Admiral, we'll be on board *The Vermillion* shortly." She gestured for Melody to cut the connection. "I understand that when we're faced with something we haven't dealt with before, it can be difficult to comprehend, but several of us have tried to explain what these ships are and he just doesn't want to understand."

"He's a soldier, Fiona," Phil said from the seat next to hers. "He understands the idea of might makes right and little beyond that. We're trying to explain that something he's used to being in control of is smarter than he is, and it's upsetting his way of thinking. There's only so much we can do about that."

"I know, Phil, I know. I just hate dealing with closed minds." She reached over and patted his hand.

"Should we land on the deck, or in the flight bay?" Del asked. "The Ruby Guard has lost enough of their drone fighters, there should be room in the flight bay." His voice was still little more than a whisper.

"The flight bay will have atmosphere," Professor Aduncus said. "Let's go there. I have already been in contact with their medical officer, who is a low-level reader. They'll meet us there to see to our wounded."

Skylar shuddered. People mostly needed medical attention due to him draining them. Sure, there were a few with sprains and bruises from the couple of rough rides they'd endured, but most of the "injured" had been nearly bled dry of their powers.

"She's also arranging for their cafeteria to be ready to receive us," the professor continued. "Food and rest is what we need the most at this point." He paused and when Skylar looked up at him, he was staring right at Skylar. "Everyone *will* recover, we just need the opportunity to do so."

Skylar heard the professor's words, and he realized his mentor was trying to make him feel better, but they knotted in his gut. They just reinforced the fact that he was the cause of their exhaustion.

"Flight bay, it is," Del said. "We'll be landing in three minutes." Then his voice rang out through the ship. "We're three minutes from landing on *The Vermillion*. Hang in there, folks—we're clear of the fighting and almost to safety."

Skylar half expected there to be a cheer, but there wasn't. As Del's voice faded, there was just silence. Silence that lasted three minutes, until Del announced they'd landed. It had been so gentle, Skylar barely registered Astara had stopped moving.

People rapidly fled the ship once the airlock opened.

As Skylar stood, figuring it might be a good thing if he could get something to eat and rest a bit, Del cleared his throat. "Skylar, do you mind bringing me something to eat?"

Skylar blinked at him for a second. "Don't you want to go find something yourself?"

Del shook his head. "Astara and I are still working out some new exterior configurations for her, and more interior changes as well. I'm actually a little surprised at how excited she is to be free of their network. It's been part of her since she was created, but we're offering her a chance to be her own ship and she wants to take it. I might have to go in search of a bathroom fairly soon, but I think we need to get some of these improvements worked out fast. She's already altered a bit so she doesn't look like the other AI fighters, but there's more we need to do. Plus, we're trying to figure out how to get the AI out of the stargate."

"Yeah, there's that too, isn't there?" Skylar rubbed his face. He wanted desperately to get some sleep. He hoped he might think a little more clearly with some shut eye. It was probably too much to hope for that the admiral would come up with a solution for the stargate that didn't involve blowing it up.

"Yeah, and I bet we have to figure it out too." Del echoed Skylar's thoughts. "Go get something to eat. It'll make you feel better. Ask Grandfather to check with the med bay and see if they have something other than stimpatches to help us stay awake for a while longer."

"Will do." When Skylar started down the corridor to the hold, he was a little surprised there weren't people still there. The past couple of times he'd been through the corridor, it had been full of people, and without them, the shiny metal walls reminded him way too much of the bigger ships, the ones that had tried to kill him. He wondered, if they were able to keep Astara, how hard it would be to get her to change the color, or if paint would stick to her without too much trouble, just so she wouldn't be so much like the killer ships.

"You're taking long enough," Solaria said as she and Leonada fell into step with Skylar at the bottom of the ramp.

"I figured you'd have been the first one to the cafeteria," Skylar said. The hanger bay smelled of grease and other chemicals he couldn't identify. It was a rough and harsh smell, but then Astara hadn't had much of a smell before everyone filled her up. Then she had smelled like… sweat and fear. Even before he had started draining people, they'd been afraid. A living ship was something new to all of them, and the other ships attacking them had made things worse.

Solaria wrapped an arm around his shoulder, giving him a side hug, yet obviously careful not to squish Filzbalm in the maneuver. "I don't need to be a feeler to tell you're stressed. You're driving Uncle Phil nuts right now. He's worried about you, but there's a lot of other people who need his help too."

"So he asked you to talk to me?" Skylar wasn't surprised Phil had picked up on his anxiety but he wished he'd been given more time to deal with it.

"Well, yeah. We're friends." She rubbed Filzbalm's head with her thumb as they walked. "We're not out of the woods yet, Skylar. We've all got to hold it together a little longer. We're Del's support network too. We crack, and he might crack. I think we're going to need him some more."

"And he's already done so much," Leonada added from Skylar's other side.

"He's running at power levels even Professor Aduncus isn't used to," Solaria said as they entered a hallway leading away from the bay. "The Professor hasn't said anything, but I think he's worried about Del. This is a new gift, and Del's not getting a chance to adjust to it. There's a chance he might burn out."

Skylar shook his head. "Not while I'm around. I'm not letting him burn out. I can't lose Del." Inside he started to crack. He stopped and leaned up against the wall, pulling out from under Solaria's arm. "I can't lose him, and I can't lose you."

Filzbalm rubbed against his check. *"You're not going to lose anyone. We're all going to be here."*

"I can't." Skylar sniffled. He was tired and he hadn't been prepared for Solaria to ambush him to talk. The tears he'd been holding back came.

Solaria hugged him. The vicious predator suddenly turned soft and caring. It was one of the things that had drawn him to her in the first place. "It's okay. We've all been through a lot, and you're shouldering a majority of the responsibility."

"And I've failed the school and Ms. Calibry," Skylar forced out through a tight throat. "We should've been faster. We should've been stronger."

Solaria rubbed his back. "Skylar, you didn't fail Ms. Calibry, I did. I couldn't get my shield up fast enough. I had the middle of us covered, but the beam got around *my* shield. There was nothing you could've done at that point." Her voice broke slightly. "But like I said back on the ship, we've got to hold it together. We're not out of this yet, just because we found a spot to catch our breath."

Skylar clung to her. He'd never considered it had been her shield—he'd just felt like it had been his idea. He'd been the one trying to keep the movers aware of their surroundings and heading the right way. "But I was the one drawing power from everyone to give to Del. I nearly killed people."

"Nearly. *Nearly*, Skylar. Note: you *didn't*. I'm sure that everyone on Astara understands that you were trying to make sure we got out of that ship alive, and we did. That's the important thing—we got out alive, and Del's made some impressive progress in getting Astara sorted out. He wouldn't have been able to do that without you getting us all focused and feeding him power."

As Solaria held him and Skylar forced himself to pull his emotions together, he wondered what it would've been like to have a sister growing up. Solaria had become close enough to him that he would've been happy to call her his family, his sister. Just like Del was the closest thing he'd had to a brother. Sure, he and Teir had been close, but maybe because they were all psychic and occasionally linking minds, Skylar felt closer to Del than he ever had to Teir.

After several minutes, his tears subsided and Skylar took a deep breath. He straightened and looked at Solaria. Her eyes were slightly red too, like she'd cried with him. "Thank you."

She smiled sadly at him. "That's what family's all about. As far as Mom, Dad and Uncle Phil are concerned, you're part of the clan. Don't you forget that. Not everyone gets invited into a Pantherian family."

He forced himself to give her a grin. "Thank you."

"Now let's go get some food. This stimpatch is wearing off and I'm getting hungry." Solaria turned him back down toward the cafeteria.

"I'm surprised you used another one after Pantheria," Leonada said, effectively changing the subject.

"Not a problem," Solaria said. "They give me a boost for a little while, but they aren't a problem. Not at all."

"I've heard of people getting addicted to them." Leonada led them around a turn and there was the cafeteria. People were lined up waiting for the food dispensers to get them what they wanted.

A quick glance was all Skylar needed to spot Professor Aduncus. He was halfway down a line. Skylar knew the professor was as tired and hungry as any of them and he hated bothering him, but he knew the professor wouldn't mind since it was for Del.

"Hold my place." He glanced at Solaria. "I need to go ask the Professor something."

"Sure, and if you take too long, I'll get something for you and Filzbalm."

"Del too," Skylar said as he hurried over to Professor Aduncus.

Professor Aduncus stood between Professor Ruff and Ms. Grissom. They were talking about something as Skylar rushed over, but grew silent when he got close.

"Professor," Skylar blurted out. "Del wanted me to ask you if you could check with the medical officer and see if you could get him something to stay awake for a while longer. We're not out of the woods yet, and he wants to be alert and ready to go. Actually, I think most of us do. But he doesn't want stimpatches, if we can avoid it."

"That might not be a bad idea," Professor Ruff said first. "Del's right, there's still more to do, but I think most of our people are going to be safer if they stay on *The Vermillion*."

"I agree," Professor Aduncus said and shoved his hands in his pockets. "I think a stimulant might be in order. Once we've had a bite to eat, I'll go investigate it. There are several safe ones designed for psychics."

Ms. Grissom shook her head, then ran her hand over her hair to straighten it back out. "If I'd been thinking, I'd have grabbed our supply on Stars' End, but there was so much else to do. Trying to decide what was important to take and what wasn't." She sighed and ran her hand through her hair again.

Skylar realized she was as stressed out about everything that was happening as he was. He'd never seen Ms. Grissom stressed about anything before. She was always on top of things and what she couldn't control, she'd manipulate until it looked like she was controlling it. For the first time since Skylar had met her, he felt he was seeing the person behind the powerful psychic mask she portrayed. It made her more human.

Skylar didn't let her know he'd seen through her, if only for a second. "Thanks, Professor. I'm going to get food for me, Filzbalm, and Del and take it back to Astara. Del wants to remain with her as he's figuring out her ins and outs. He thinks he can help her appear less like an AI ship."

"That's probably a good thing," Professor Aduncus said. "Tell him not to push it. We all need to be at our best before the next shoe drops."

"I will." Skylar glanced around. Solaria and Leonada were nearly up to their turn at the food dispensers, and luckily there wasn't anyone behind them. He was able to rejoin them without feeling like he was cutting in line, even if he had asked them to save his place.

He wanted to get through the rest of the day without upsetting anyone else, if he could help it. He wondered what the professors had been talking about. He was a little worried it had been him or Del, but he decided not to dwell on it as he got their food and headed back to the ship. Solaria was there with him as he walked back, and that made him feel good. He wasn't alone.

19
Ramifications And Fear

SKYLAR WASN'T sure if it was luck or ship design, but a large bathroom was just inside the landing bay corridor. It made getting there quickly easy, particularly since Del and Astara were still trying to figure out the best way to get basic humanoid luxuries created. The thing was, they had bigger problems to worry about.

After almost a day, there were still AI ships around them. Some of the ships had managed to complete their mitosis and the Ruby Guard was doing their best to block the smaller ships from getting near the stargate. The admiral didn't really seem to care that Skylar and Del— actually Del and Melody, but Skylar felt like he, Solaria and Filzbalm were part of things too—knew more about the AI ships than he did, or than Ms. Grissom did, and she was the only person from their group he seemed interested in talking to.

That meant Skylar ended up being a go-between for Ms. Grissom and Del. Although Ms. Grissom was a strong enough reader to reach Del's mind easily, she claimed that since his new powers had developed she was having trouble understanding everything Del said. Since Professor Aduncus hadn't reported anything like that, Skylar wasn't sure what she was going on about. Solaria figured it was just Ms. Grissom, being Ms. Grissom, or trying to put on some kind of face for the admiral. They also didn't seem to want to use coms to relay information.

Regardless of the reason, the running back and forth from Astara to the admiral's ready room, and even the bridge of *The Vermillion,* was giving him lots of time to get familiar with the war cruiser. It was the biggest ship Skylar had ever been on, and in some ways, it was harder to get around on than Stars' End had been. There were a lot more people there too. A fair number of them were from species he didn't instantly recognize, like the large fish who floated along the halls in a bubble of water. When he described him to Del, his friend had explained that the man had most likely been a Resmordian, a non-humanoid inhabitant of Tursipia, and with what they had learned on Pantheria, possibly the original inhabitants.

More dramatic than Skylar's reaction to some of the occupants of *The Vermilion* was their reaction to Filzbalm. It didn't seem to matter if the Solar Drake was on Skylar's shoulder or flying along beside him, people stopped and stared. The other students on Stars' End had gotten used to seeing him after Skylar returned from Armstrong's Ring with the little guy, but on the battle cruiser, he was new and unusual. Several times, Skylar had been stopped and asked about him. If he'd had time, he'd answered a couple questions, but normally he asked them to stop in at Astara, and if he was available, he'd talk.

As he hurried down the final corridor before getting to the bridge, Skylar felt a heightened level of excitement coming from the large room. He picked up his pace to see what was going on.

Filzbalm landed on his shoulder, as Admiral Temer found the Solar Drake flying around his bridge to be a distraction. *"I think we're about to win."*

"Really?" The news surprised Skylar, as the AI ships were proving quick to adapt. They changed their fighting tactics every few minutes, and figured out how to modulate their shields in various ways to block the fleet's weapons. The larger ships seemed faster to adapt than the fighters and Skylar wondered if they'd been built with larger processors or something similar.

They'd learned from Astara that the AI ships all had central processors, and for the personality of the ships to remain intact they had to have a physical home, like her central column. It was possible for an AI to just be data for a short period of time. Del was working out if that was what had taken over the stargate, and not a virus. Naturally, the Admiral was still fighting against that idea.

The door slid open and revealed the bridge. It was a collection of workstations with a huge viewscreen that showed the space in whatever direction the cameras were pointed at the time. Currently, they faced the opening stargate, where more fighters and cruisers were coming through.

"We've got reinforcements coming in, but that's not a guaranteed win," Skylar said as the door closed behind him.

"But it does improve our odds," Filzbalm countered and Skylar couldn't argue.

Ms. Grissom was seated at one of the workstations near the Admiral's station. Skylar hurried over to her.

"What does Del have to say?" she asked, acknowledging Skylar's presence.

"They're still working on a way to figure out the next shield frequency the ships are going to deploy," Skylar said as he sat on the edge of her worktop. He was careful not to touch any part of the touchscreen and possibly disrupt what she was hard at work on. "Astara says the ships normally use a randomized algorithm when they are cycling their shields. She did say it takes them approximately five minutes to make the adjustments."

Admiral Temer, who sat on the other side of Ms. Grissom, grinned. "We can work with five minutes. We might only get in a blow or two between shield modulations, but with the fresh guns showing up, we can make that work." He stood and hurried over to the weapons officer's station.

"Why don't you stay here for a few minutes, Skylar?" Ms. Grissom suggested. "No telling when he's going to want something else answered." She shook her head. "I'd forgotten how focused these military types can be. I advise that you never go into service. I don't think you have the personality for it."

"If it means listening to every stupid thing narrow-minded people have to suggest, then I think you're right." He was trying his best to keep his opinions of the amount of blind following he saw from the people on the ship to himself, but when he was given an opening like Ms. Grissom just offered him, he took it.

She gave him a rare smile.

"All right," the admiral said as he came back over. "My people are passing that along to the rest of the fleet. The new guys are raring to go on these ships. Let's hope this works. It might be a little while before we know. Why don't you go relax a little?" He waved Ms. Grissom toward the door.

She stood with a sigh. Tiredness rolled off her like a heavy odor. It made Skylar wonder if she'd had any rest. Some of the group from the school were resorting to artificial stimulants to stay on their feet; others were taking naps as they could. He couldn't remember seeing Ms. Grissom doing either. Skylar had grabbed a couple of naps when people weren't needing him.

Once they were off the bridge and the door closed, he touched her arm. "You look like you need a nap or more."

She smiled weakly. "You're becoming a remarkable young man. Thank you for worrying about me. I'm going to get something to eat and see if that helps. If it doesn't, then maybe the admiral will give me some down time while they get your latest suggestion worked out. I'm actually surprised the president would send her elite troops to our aid. I figured the space marines or something, but not the Ruby Guard. Someone pulled some major strings to get them here. I wish I knew who, but I'm too tired to think about that right now. Get some rest, Skylar."

"I'm heading back to Astara to relax there, in case Del needs anything." They reached an intersection and Skylar headed toward the hanger.

"Skylar, have you seen Professor Aduncus recently?" Her question stopped him in his tracks.

"I think he was going to find a spot to get a quick nap," Skylar replied. "Try the guest quarters."

"After I get something to eat, I will." She turned and headed away from him.

Skylar thought it was strange she wasn't using her telepathy or her coms to try to find Professor Aduncus. She was strong enough that finding him should've been relatively easy.

Once they were a short distance from the bridge, Filzbalm took off and spent the rest of their walk back to Astara circling Skylar's head. He always stayed a couple of inches away, so he didn't bump into Skylar as they made their way down the corridor. After spending way too much time cooped up in Skylar's envirosuit's helmet, he was happy to get out and fly.

As Skylar entered the hanger bay, he was surprised to see that Astara had changed color. She was no longer a bright shiny metal ship, but dulled, and almost blue. When he went up the ramp and into the airlock, open on both ends to make it easier for people to come and go, he realized the inside of the ship was no longer shiny too. It was almost a sky blue. The effect was much more comforting.

"So, what do you think?" Del asked as Skylar walked into the control room.

"Nice color. Much better than the shiny, raw-metal look." Skylar took the seat that was quickly becoming his. It was next to Del's and had its own interface screen. "I thought you were working on how to get to the AI in the stargate, and environmental changes were going to have to wait."

Del sighed and scratched his chin. "I was getting burned out on that. Melody went to get us both something to eat, and I figured I could see about making some simple cosmetic changes. We're going to have to find Astara some mass she can absorb before we do much more than just change colors. These fighters are fairly light on everything but their central core, their guns, and their shields. Still trying to work out how their propulsion system works. It's almost like it's some kind of organic system and I don't totally understand it, other than she gathers random atoms as she flies through space and converts them into power."

"That doesn't sound like anything she would've learned from Sol Three," Skylar mused.

"No. I haven't said much about this yet, but the AIs have been picking up tech as they encounter other species." Del brought up something on his screen. "That's why a lot of it is strange to us. This is her main weapons diagram. The basic configuration is similar to human weapons from a few hundred years ago, but the power source is different. Some kind of crystalline base."

"Is that why they're slow, but really effective?" Skylar studied the picture. He wasn't a weapon's expert, but he knew the basics—almost every kid did, particularly those who played Galactic Explorers like he and Teir had. One of the biggest quest chains had been gathering the parts for a spaceship, and they'd included weapons on theirs. He recognized the initial design, but like Del said, the power source was odd. It wasn't routed directly into Astara's systems, but seemed to be isolated with a backup system that was probably for recharging that connected into her power network.

"Probably. When we have time and more resources, I'm going to see about bringing her tech up to modern and see where that gets us. We can probably make her propulsion system more efficient with an upgrade too."

"So, we're keeping her?" Skylar was fairly sure they were going to do everything they could to keep Astara, but other than a few vague discussions, nobody had come out and said it.

"I think at this point, even if we have to go to some sleazy forger in the Galaxeria and get them to make papers for us, we're going to keep her." Del put a hand on the central column. "I'm not about to let the corps get their grubby hands on her and dissect her. She's alive. She's different, like we are, but she's alive, and we need to keep her that way. Grandfather said he's going to do what he can to slip her away from the fleet without too many questions. Right now, as far as the admiral is concerned, she's an experimental ship from school. Grandfather said he thinks that's probably the best way to handle this."

"Do we know what Ms. Grissom is thinking about this?" Skylar could just see the school counselor throwing a wrench into things.

"Don't know. I think the Admiral is keeping her busy right now."

"Yeah, me too." The smell of food drew Skylar's attention down the hall as Melody came into the control room carrying food for her and Del.

"Hey, Skylar, if I'd known you were going to be back so soon, I'd have gotten something for you and Filzbalm." She set the two boxes of food down on one of the vacant chairs.

"We're good for another hour or so," Skylar said.

"The folks in the cafeteria were going on about reinforcements coming through the stargate and that everything's going to be over soon." Melody took one of the boxes and opened it so she could start eating.

"They think so," Skylar said. The sight and smell of the food made him think he needed to go get food sooner rather than later.

"Food is always a good thing," Filzbalm said from his shoulder. The Solar Drake yawned. *"Wake me when you're ready to eat."*

"These ships went down pretty easy at first," Del said, "But they learn quickly. I hope the information about the five-minute cycling is helpful."

"The admiral seemed to think it would be." Skylar tapped on his screen and brought up the display that showed the space around them. One of the larger AI ships exploded into small bits as a squadron of Ruby Guard fighters soared through its remains. There were still several of the larger ships and a bunch of the smaller ones to deal with.

A lot of the smaller ones were trying to slip past the blockade the Ruby Guard had set up at the stargate. They were nothing if not determined. They probably understood that they didn't have the speed to make a run for it across the system and the modern ships would chase them into the ground. Skylar stopped himself and smiled. He was thinking like a hunter; Solaria would be pleased.

"I'm worried it will only work for so long." Del got out of his seat and retrieved his box. "The admiral doesn't seem to understand how fast an AI can learn and adapt to a changing situation."

"I think the admiral doesn't understand a lot of things," Melody said between bites. "But he knows if he can blow it out of the sky, he's right. Mother hates these military types and despises that Father has to deal with them on a regular basis. He's in pretty deep with all of them, particularly the Ruby Guard. Only the best for the president"

It was the first time Skylar could remember Melody talking about her father. He knew her mother ran the largest beauty corp in the galaxy, and he couldn't imagine that someone running a beauty corp would need to deal with military types on a regular basis. He was about to ask her when Solaria dashed in.

"Skylar, Professor Aduncus is looking for you," she heaved.

"Why hasn't he mentally called me?" Skylar asked.

"Or used the coms?" Melody echoed.

"Something weird is going on, not sure what." Solaria pointed out the door. "He's in the guest meeting room."

"Does it have a food dispenser?" Skylar stared down the corridor. "Filzbalm's hungry."

"I think I saw one in there," Solaria said, and sat on the closest chair.

Skylar stopped and turned back to her. It wasn't like her to be that out of breath. "Are you okay?"

With her head bent over her knees, she nodded. "Just ran too fast to get here. I'll catch my breath and be fine."

"Okay." She didn't look okay, she looked a bit strung out, but he didn't push it. He didn't have time. He had to respond to the professor's summons.

When he reached the guest meeting room, Professor Aduncus was there, along with Ms. Grissom, Phil, and Professor Ruff. Professor Aduncus had obviously had a fair amount of rest—he looked better than he had since they landed on *The Vermilion*. Ms. Grissom was eating something from a bowl, and Phil was sitting attentively at her side with a bowl of his own. Professor Ruff looked like he could fall asleep at any moment.

"Ah, Mr. Mars. Please, come in and have a seat." Professor Aduncus waved him toward the table.

"Do you mind if I make use of the food dispenser first?" Skylar spotted it on the wall behind the table.

"Of course, go ahead." Professor Aduncus chuckled. "I think we've all been running pretty close to empty this past day."

"Yeah." Skylar hurried over as he didn't want to keep the teachers and Phil waiting. He got Filzbalm's raw meat first, then got himself a burger. From the last one he'd tried, he knew it wouldn't be as good as the ones Solaria's mom had cooked for him, but it would suffice to get him through.

As Filzbalm started eating, Skylar settled in a cushioned chair that was a lot more comfortable than the basic metal ones on Astara. "What's going on?" he asked after he finished chewing the first bite of his burger. It was as bland as he'd figured it would be. "Solaria didn't say. I figure it can't be too horrible, since you didn't send me a mental message."

Professor Aduncus nodded slowly. "Skylar, we need to talk about your ability to draw people into a gestalt."

"Gestalt—that's where I'm accessing other people's powers and fueling Del?" The burger was suddenly tasting a lot worse—Professor Aduncus rarely used his first name when things were official, and the gathering around the table felt fairly official.

"A gestalt is when a reader connects multiple people and then takes control of them. The people you tap into lose a part of themselves while you have control of them." Professor Aduncus stood and started pacing. That made Skylar more nervous. "Although you are continually surprising us with the depth of your powers, this isn't something you should be able to do on your own."

Skylar nodded. "It started on Pantheria, when Solaria's Aunt Blizza was using the crystal claw to imprison Freyandor. Someone needed to finish up what she started and from the moment I first met her, she'd called me the 'light.' She gave me the crystal claw to be the focus of everyone there. If we hadn't worked together, we never would've succeeded." Skylar set down his burger and looked at his palm. "The claw exploded. A shard of crystal went into my hand."

Phil reached for Skylar's hand and looked at it. "There's no scar. It hasn't been long enough for there not to be a scar."

"I heal fast." Skylar shrugged as Phil released his hand. "When I've been focusing everyone's power for Del, the crystal's been burning in my hand, almost like the power is going through it first and then out to Del."

Professor Aduncus pursed his lips and nodded. "Artifacts. Apparently, this crystal claw is…*was* a psychic artifact. There aren't many of them around. They were created to help amplify our powers. They make us more than we are."

"And less," Professor Ruff grumbled. "I've dealt with artifacts before. They can be very dangerous."

"As we've all experienced, thanks to Skylar," Ms. Grissom agreed as she finished her soup and pushed the bowl toward the center of the table.

Skylar was confused. Sure, he'd come close to killing people, but something in Ms. Grissom's tone made it sound worse than that. "I don't understand."

Ms. Grissom sighed. "Skylar, you're a good young man, and you've been through a lot these past few months. Grown more than any of us would've expected. But in that growth, you've also become dangerous, and some people are concerned."

"What people?" Skylar didn't want to touch his burger anymore.

Filzbalm also abandoned his meat and flew to Skylar's shoulder in an obvious show of solidarity.

"That really doesn't matter at this point." Aduncus flashed a hard look at Ms. Grissom as if telling her to be quiet. "Skylar, we all know that what happened when we escaped the ship stressed you out. It taxed all of our abilities to their limits, and I think most of us would do it again if the situation returned. But more than a few of the passengers on Astara have never experienced power on that level before, and it scared them."

Skylar slumped in his chair, thinking about how few people from Stars' End had returned to Astara once they reached *the Vermillion*. Phil and Professor Aduncus had come, besides Solaria, Leonada, and Melody. Beyond that, no one else had approached the hanger bay that he'd noticed. He hadn't stopped to think about what he'd done—beyond the fact that he'd nearly killed people. He'd been trying to do what Solaria said and push it aside until there was a better time and place to deal with it.

He shook his head. "I didn't want to do it. I was just doing what I thought I had to so that Del and Astara would have the power to break free of the big AI ship."

Professor Aduncus nodded. "I understand that. I think that, like Del's ability to talk to the AIs, this is a new power for you, and one you didn't ever expect to have once you let go of the crystal claw. But the artifact didn't let go of you. Why didn't you tell anyone about it?"

Skylar shrugged. "It didn't seem important. The wound healed quickly and there was so much to do after the amount of destruction Freyandor caused on Pantheria, I had other things to worry about. If it got to be a problem, hurting, itching or something I figured I could go to the nurse after I got back to school, but that's not going to happen now, is it?"

"Not for a while, at least," Ms. Grissom said with a sigh. "Skylar, we need to ask you to not use the crystal again until we have a chance to study it. We should try to remove it from your hand."

"But when are we going to be able to do that?" Skylar did his best to push down the indignation he was feeling. There was so much going on—they were still in the middle of a war with the AI ships. They didn't have time to worry about him until that was all over. And none of them had talked about what was going to happen to the students, particularly him, the orphan of the group. Although he doubted Phil and the Unicas would let anything happen to him, he didn't know that for sure.

"There hasn't been any down time," Phil said. "You're right. Since that night, you've been going non-stop, and from the looks of things, it may be a while before they slow down any at all. We just need you to be careful when you use your powers, particularly if it's your reader gift."

Skylar huffed. "Would it make you all happy if I got a dampening bracelet again? Would that make me less dangerous?"

"We don't want that," Professor Aduncus said. "Right now, we need all of us at our peak performance, and I, for one, know you hadn't meant to do what you did. You were trying to save us all. We all understand that."

"I don't think you realize everything you did when you were pulling our power from us," Ms. Grissom said.

Some of his bluster disappeared. "Phil told me I almost killed people."

Professor Ruff nodded. "There was that, but for some of the more delicate talents, it was more than that."

Skylar wondered how there could be more than nearly killing people. "What more?"

Ms. Grissom closed her eyes. "Some of us are having trouble recovering."

"Recovering?" A sickening feeling filled Skylar. He'd been wondering the real reason Ms. Grissom wasn't using her reader talent to communicate with any of them. Had he done something to her powers? Was that what they were trying to say? Not only had he almost killed people, but he'd drained them to the point their powers were permanently damaged?

"My powers are still here. I can't access them without extreme pain." Ms. Grissom rubbed her head. "I keep thinking that I only need some rest, and without Principal Fuspatula here, I'm in charge of the delegation from Stars' End. Admiral Temer isn't giving me much chance of that. Several other people are also reporting lingering effects, mostly readers and feelers."

"So far, no movers are reporting problems," Professor Ruff added. "Although we are all exhausted, even after having time to rest and recover physically."

"We all know that exaggerated use of our powers can have these effects," Professor Aduncus said. "To be fair, we haven't had nearly the time resting we need. It'll be a few days before we know the full extent." He walked over and put a hand on Skylar's shoulder. "We don't want to worry you, but there was no way to tell you to not use this gift without laying it all out for you. I'm sorry we've added to your burden right now."

"They're all very worried," Filzbalm said.

Skylar hadn't needed him to tell him that. He could feel it easily. Professor Aduncus was the only one in the room not projecting fear and concern, although Phil's was a mixed emotion. It was like he was more worried about Ms. Grissom getting back to normal than Skylar hurting more people. But he was also worried about

Skylar, and Skylar couldn't tell exactly what that was about.

Letting out a long sigh, Skylar nodded. "I understand. I think. Timing isn't good, but you had to deal with it before it got out of control. I never meant to hurt anyone. I just wanted to help Del get us all to safety." He felt like he was repeating himself, but he couldn't think of anything better to say. That was all he had and it didn't feel like it was nearly enough. He was either going to have to get the crystal removed, or find a way to control it so he wasn't a complete menace to those around him. But first, they had to finish the fight with the AIs, and if Del was right, even with the reinforcements, that wasn't going to be easy.

20
Fighting The Data

SKYLAR HAD almost gotten back to the hanger bay when the alarm claxons went off. Although he'd been asked to not use his powers unless absolutely necessary, they'd become almost reflex. He reached out to Del as he took off running the last little distance. *"What's going on?"*

"One of the big ships broke through the blockade and is making a run for the stargate," Del replied. *"It's got several fighters with it."*

"It'll never fit," Skylar said as he ran up the ramp.

"But it might be able to get close enough to block it until it can make itself small enough to make it," Del said. *"Or it could block things until the fighters can get through. Astara says that after the reinforcements arrived, there's been enough openings of the gate that the AI there can probably operate it."*

"That's not good." Skylar dropped to regular speech as he sped into the control room.

"Right," Del agreed.

"So we need to stop the fighters from getting through," Solaria said. "And blow up the big ship before it gets too close to the gate."

"'Cause blowing it up too close to the gate might damage the gate too," Skylar finished for her. They all knew what would happen if the gate was damaged or destroyed. They would likely either be stuck in a system that wasn't overly hospitable to humanoids, or spend years getting to the next gate so they could make it home, where ever they decided that was.

"So, we need to move out," Leonada said, drawing Skylar's attention to her where she sat on the floor against the wall, like she was trying to stay out of the way.

"But can we do more than Ruby Guard?" Melody asked as she worked her interface at the central column. "I mean, sure, Astara has the same guns and shields as the fighters and the big ship, but that doesn't necessarily give us an advantage if they start modulating their shields and all."

Del chuckled. "Astara thinks she might be able to override their shields."

"What?" Skylar and Solaria said in unison.

"Wait a minute," Melody said. "If she can get around their shields, could she send data to them without rejoining their network?"

"At this point, their network isn't as strong as it used to be," Del said. He tapped something on his screen, and a display appeared on the wall on the other side of the column. He looked rather pleased with himself. "I haven't been able to get an external viewscreen working, but it wasn't that hard to get her to create a big screen for me." The scene was the two opposing fleets, or what remained of them.

Del walked over and started pointing to things Skylar already could identify. "Okay. From what we can tell, there's only three of the big ships left. The two that didn't hit the blockade seem to be trying to engage the heavy cruisers that aren't part of the wall. Our fighters are doing a number on them. Looks like about half of their shots are getting through as the ships work to modulate their shields, but they aren't fast enough. Their fighters appear to be split between the ships drawing fire and the one making a run for it. The fighters hitting the blockade are fast and agile, and seem to be doing a lot of damage to our ships.”

“Like they did when the guard first arrived,” Skylar said, studying the display.

“Right,” Del agreed. “But now, they’ve had time to learn our tactics, or at least, the military’s tactics.”

“But we don’t play by military rules.” Solaria grinned as she walked over to the display. “You haven’t had time to upgrade Astara’s drive, have you?”

“I can only do so much,” Del said. “And that’s going to take materials. I didn’t want her absorbing part of *The Vermillion*. I think it would probably upset Admiral Temer.”

“And heavens forbid we upset the Admiral.” Leonada came over too.

“So what do we do?” Skylar asked.

“We leave the *Vermillion* and head for their ship,” Melody said. “We get Astara to break the shields of one of their vessels, and we dump a virus into their systems. I’ve been working on something while Del and Astara have been busy with everything else. I’ve come up with a virus that should attack their base code and destabilize it, at least long enough for us to finish off the ships before they can get into the stargate.”

“What about the one in the stargate?” Solaria asked. “We’ve got to take it out too.”

“I’m not sure this will work on that one. If it’s integrated itself into the gate’s systems, it may have altered its base codes, and this virus will be useless on it.” Melody sent an image to the screen, and it took up about half the screen. It looked like a bunch of lines of computer code that Skylar didn’t understand.

“But if it’s still connected to their network, the virus might cause it to malfunction,” Del said. “As long as it doesn’t fry the gate, we can go with a malfunction.”

“Maybe.” Melody didn’t sound real confident.

"Let's find out after we take down the other ships." Skylar stepped away from the wall. "We should let Professor Aduncus know about this before we leave." He sighed. "I'm already in hot water with the professors—I don't want to make this worse."

"I'll let him know," Del said.

Skylar shook his head. "Let me." He tentatively reached out for the professor. *"Professor?"*

Through the connection, Skylar could hear the claxons continuing to go off. He'd stopped hearing them once he got in Astara. *"Mr. Mars, you're supposed to be limiting your use of your powers."*

"I know. Look, this is important, and we don't have much time. Del and Melody have a plan, but we're going to have to take Astara out to implement it." He quickly projected the whole plan to the professor. *"We've got to move fast so the gate isn't destroyed."*

"Give Phil and me time to get there. I will alert Ms. Grissom and Admiral Temer of the basics of the plan, since we don't have time to get complicated. Get the ship...Astara, ready to go."

"Thank you." There was a feeling of confidence coming off the Professor. It made Skylar feel good. After the meeting with the professors, he wasn't sure any of them would trust him again. But in that instant, he knew Professor Aduncus understood who he was at a level Skylar probably wasn't even aware of. Realizing that made Skylar even surer they were going to come out of everything just fine.

"Professor Aduncus and Phil want to go with us. They'll be here shortly." He walked over and took his seat. He could still see the big screen, and that made him feel a little better about what they were about to do. Having Professor Aduncus and Phil with them made him feel like their success was almost guaranteed.

"That'll give me a little more time to tweak this virus," Melody said and she worked feverishly at her station a few feet away.

Sitting there in his seat, Skylar looked around the barren room, occupied by just the dozen seats and the central column with its interface panels. The addition of the big screen was a major improvement. "So Del, do you think if we get through all this, we can get some more comfortable seats in here? If we're going to keep Astara, we need to make her biped-friendly."

Del hurried over to his seat. "As soon as we get the raw materials and I can show her how to make what we need, we'll get on it."

"Good. That will make life easier."

"I think it might be a good idea for all of us to get into our envirosuits, just in case," Phil said as he and Professor Aduncus rushed in. "If Astara's hull is breached in this fighting, we'll need things ready to protect us."

From the tone of his voice, there wasn't going to be any arguing with him, as he was already heading back into the corridor that led to the hold where they'd left their suits and helmets. Ignoring Filzbalm's complaints about going back into the helmet, Skylar moved as fast as he could so they could get out of the hanger.

As they left the hanger, their coms beeped.

"Grandfather, where are you going?" Click asked.

"Click, is the Cosmos's ship with you?" Professor Aduncus asked.

"Yes," Click responded, "a couple of minutes behind me. They were slowed down by having a tether on *Rescue Paw One*."

"Drop the tether on the *Paw*," Phil said. "I'll contact Admiral Temer and have her towed the rest of the way in. You two can follow us. We could use the extra fire power."

"What are we doing?" Connor came over the coms. "Mom's ready to get off the ship for a while so she can stretch her legs."

"We're ending this fight," Skylar said. "Fall in with us and we'll explain on the way."

"Roger that," Connor said.

"Will do," Click replied.

"Professor Aduncus, or whoever is manning *the Astara*, please come in," a female voice said over the coms.

Skylar glanced at the professor, who nodded.

"This is Aduncus. How can I help you?"

"Admiral Temer asked me to advise you that he is routing a squadron of fighters to accompany you. He wishes you success and the fighters will do what they can to guard you as you engage the enemy at the gate."

The professor smiled slightly. "We appreciate the admiral's assistance in this." Then he gestured for Melody to cut the connection. "Looks like Ms. Grissom got us some help. Hopefully they'll make things easier, not just get in the way."

"Yeah." Skylar had seen the admiral and his soldiers in action, and he figured the chances were high they'd be in the way more than they'd be helpful, but as they'd proven so far in fighting the AI ships, every gun was needed. A squadron of fighters would definitely help more than just the *Diver* and the *Gold* could. It also improved the chances they would all make it back alive.

It surprised Skylar that they didn't encounter any resistance from the fighters who'd slipped through the blockade with the larger vessel. They all seemed intent on reaching the stargate and getting through. The Ruby Guard fighters moved quickly to cut them off, but even taking advantage of the shield modulation flaw, they still struggled to keep the fighters from reaching the gate.

"How is this going to work?" Skylar asked as they drew close enough that Astara could disrupt the bigger ship's shields.

"We're going to take down her shields," Melody explained, "then send a stream of data, with the virus in it, to the ship. It will take us about thirty seconds to get the transmission complete. Unfortunately, we'll also be defenseless during that time as Astara's shields are also going to have to be down."

"The big problem is going to be blocking the ship and the rest of the network from trying to take us out," Del took over the discussion. "The network has had time to reform after our assault yesterday. We're going to have to block them while Melody sends the virus over. That's also when we'll be in need of coverage from the ships around us. I'm not sure Astara and I can fire our weapons while we're fighting on the mental plane."

"I wish one of us could be firing the weapons," Solaria said.

Del grinned. "We might have time to set that up. Astara just informed me that we could reroute weapons control to an interface."

As he spoke, another interface touchscreen appeared in the side of the column. A seat rose out of the floor for an operator to sit at.

Solaria smiled so hard, she flashed fangs. "I've got this. I presume it's a fairly straight-forward firing control."

"Correct," Del said. "Skylar, I know you're not supposed to be linking a lot of people together right now." Del glanced at his grandfather before he continued. "I'm hoping that with just a short fight, we can get by with just you and Filzbalm augmenting me and Astara."

Thankful for something useful to do, Skylar nodded. "Of course. As soon as you're ready, we are."

"Always," Filzbalm said from Skylar's helmet.

"Good." Del glanced at the big screen, showing them nearing the AI ship that was almost to the stargate. "I'm glad those bigger ships are fairly slow."

"But they're deadly," Solaria said. "If we get too close to it, we'll need to take out its weaponry and do enough damage so that it can't rebuild right away."

"Exactly." Del glanced from the big screen down to his interface screen. "Shield coming up in fifteen seconds. Astara is already working on bringing it down."

From the view on Skylar's screen, they weren't slowing as they approached the ship's shield. Astara must be very confident she would be able to bring the ship's first line of defense down. Skylar gripped the sides of his chair as they reached the point where they should impact the shields. When they past that point, he let out a long breath, feeling slightly light-headed.

"She's good to her word," Del said. "Now, Skylar, link up with us. This is where things are going to get rough."

"We've got incoming AI fighters," Solaria announced. "I should have weapon's lock on them soon."

"That's good," Del replied. "Skylar, Filzbalm, Astara, and I are going into the network link to keep the ships from realizing what we're really up to."

Skylar didn't need to be told twice—over the recent days, it was becoming almost second nature to slip into a link with Del and Astara. The mental scape was different this time. A tall, lanky, dark haired young woman who looked like a cross between Del and Melody stood next to Del. She wore a simple black jump suit that looked a lot like their envirosuits.

"Astara?" Skylar asked as he closed the distance between them.

"It's nice to properly meet you, Skylar Mars," she replied. "Del Aduncus and Melody Porsche explained that a figure like your own makes it easier to communicate."

"And she's a fast learner," Del added. "Now, let's give these AIs something to think about beyond what Melody is doing to them."

"Lead on," Skylar said.

Del's form shimmered and combat armor appeared. It was sleek modern polymetallic armor favored by soldiers across the galaxy. Astara did the same, so Skylar summoned some of his own. His practice sessions with Professor Aduncus were proving handy—he'd learned to create various things on the mental plane, things that could help him when he needed extra protection, or more focused weapons than simply blasting energy at something.

Skylar made his armor as dark as Del's, copying it piece by piece. He did it so that if the AIs were trying to decide where to direct their attack, they would have to choose between two identical targets. Filzbalm blended into Skylar's armor, looking like a dark lump on his shoulder, the only difference between the two of them.

Astara led the assault. She dove into the green and black river that represented the AI's network. It was a dangerous move, but it got their attention as she created mental dams to block the river and interrupt the network.

Del hit the ship closest to them, the one closing in on the stargate. The AI had obviously learned from the network and the ships they had battled earlier. It came at them looking like a tank, its huge gun firing.

"Upload has started," Melody said in the real world. Her voice was a distant whisper, but it was enough to give Skylar an idea about how long they were going to need to keep the AI busy. Unfortunately, time moved a little differently in the mindscape than it did in the physical world.

As Del waded into the fray with the AI, Skylar did too. Del had a huge sword he swung and forced the AI back as if it were surprised at his change in tactics. Del followed it, pushing it farther back and making it move away from Astara as she continued to battle the network. Standing in the middle of it didn't seem like a good idea to Skylar, but she seemed to be holding her own as it splashed against her defenses without any obvious damage.

Skylar stuck with Del, conjuring his own sword out of his thoughts and bringing it to bear against the AI. The enemy machine intelligence created a shield in both hands, defending against their blows. It then quickly changed the shields to swords. It swung hard at Del and Skylar simultaneously, moving faster than any flesh-and-blood opponent could.

Skylar focused on the sword coming at him. Filzbalm gave him extra power to block the heavy blow. It hurt his arms as it shook through his sword. Skylar tried to counterattack, but the AI blocked every blow he swung. Del wasn't faring much better. The AI seemed more than capable of blocking them, even if they did keep causing it to step back.

"Twenty five percent," Melody said in the distance.

As Skylar continued to rain blows down on his side of the AI, Del matched him blow for blow. The AI continued to back up, then suddenly stopped. It was like it was suddenly drawing power from something—or someone. Its deep-set eyes glowed behind its own helm. Skylar got a sick feeling in the depths of his stomach and suddenly wished Solaria was there with them on the mental plane as opposed to working Astara's weapons to defend them in the physical world. She was the better fighter and always would be. He was just doing things he'd done in video games and hoping they worked in real life situations.

"Astara, is some of the network getting past you?" Del shouted as their attacks grew less and less effective.

"It's trying." Astara sounded strained. "I think I've got it blocked again."

The AI's eyes stopped glowing and the attacks once again seemed to stress it.

This was a much harder battle than any one of them could've hoped to win at. The AIs learned too fast and could react with speed that flesh-and-blood brains could never achieve. Skylar tried to increase the frequency of his attacks, but his arms were starting to ache.

"Fifty percent," Melody said.

Filzbalm launched himself off Skylar's shoulder and flew at the AI. The little Solar Drake breathed fire, causing the AI to bring his swords up to try to fend him off.

It gave Skylar and Del both openings. They struck hard and fast, nearly cleaving the AI's mental body in half at the waist. It staggered backward, dropping its arms. The swords vanished as it put its hands over the wounds and they began to close.

"Not good," Del said, and hacked at the thing's arms.

Skylar aimed his blows at the thing's head. Chips and sparks flew around as they assaulted the AI. Del succeeded in hacking off its lower arm, which immediately began to regrow. Skylar's hits on its head seemed to have similar effects, but while it was re-growing parts, it was distracted, even if those distractions were only lasting seconds.

"The network is trying to reform," Astara got out in a gasp.

Skylar risked a quick glance in her direction. The network had made major strides in getting its connection to the ship reestablished. There was only a short distance in the green stream that was separated.

"Del, help Astara. Filzbalm and I can handle this guy." Skylar started alternating which side he was swinging at. The technique was more than slightly awkward and there was no way he could do it at the speed he and Del had been striking, but he had to keep the thing occupied a few seconds longer. Melody had to be nearly done.

Del rushed out of Skylar's view, leaving him and Filzbalm to continue their assault. Filzbalm continued to make his flying, fire-breathing attacks. They seemed more effective than Skylar's hack-and-slash technique.

"Seventy-five percent," Melody called out. She sounded farther away than she had the previous times.

With a deep breath, trying to fight the fatigue that was setting into his arms, chest, and legs, Skylar continued swinging. Seeing how well Filzbalm's attacks were working, Skylar decided to change tactics. He stepped back and made his sword change to a plasma rifle. He aimed at the AI, pulled the trigger and held it as he visualized a continual stream of plasma hitting the AI.

Between his attack and Filzbalm's, the AI was engulfed in fire. Its outside melted. The AI dropped to its knees and screamed. The sound was like gears grinding before they flew apart.

Skylar's head throbbed, and he suddenly realized why a lot of readers relied on physical weapons when doing mental combat. By using a plasma rifle, he was pouring his own reserves out to attack the AI. He wasn't sure how Filzbalm was finding the energy to continue his flaming attack, but Skylar grew lightheaded and dropped to his knees.

"Ninety percent," Melody's voice was the fainted whisper rolling across the mental plane.

"Skylar, look out!" Del and Filzbalm shouted together. An arc of power lashed across the mental landscape, striking the AI and causing it to stumble back.

In its hands was a new sword. From the way its arm was raised, it had been about to strike Skylar.

Forcing himself to stand, Skylar created another sword of his own. It was the last dregs of his power. The crystal in his hand tingled, as if urging him to reach out to the power of the other people in Astara. There would be enough there for him to finish the AI—except he didn't want to finish the AI, just keep it occupied long enough for Melody to finish loading the virus that was nearly done. He only had to hold out a few seconds more and then they could all go back to their physical forms and rest. There was only so much more he could do. Skylar swung the sword, struggling to keep the point up.

"Ninety-five percent," Melody's voice was almost too faint to hear, but Skylar knew he only needed to get in a couple more blows. Filzbalm only needed another blast or two of fire. It was almost over. Everything became a blur. His thoughts were on just surviving. He had to buy them a few more seconds. The sword hit the AI's flaming body. The impact made his arms hurt even more. Sparks and bits of flaming AI flew around him. One of them landed on his armor and started to burn through.

"Ninety-eight percent." The voice was so faint, Skylar wasn't sure he'd even heard it. There was a good chance his exhausted brain was just imagining it. He swung again. The collision of the sword against the AI was so hard he nearly lost his grip on the weapon.

Filzbalm landed on his shoulder, and Skylar felt stronger. He attacked again, this time cleaving through the AI's arm.

"Ninety-nine percent." The whispered voice was definitely Melody's.

They were nearly there. He swung with all his might. The sword hit the AI and stuck.

"What?" Skylar pulled as hard as he could and he couldn't get the sword out of the AI's armor.

"You are nothing, human," the AI shouted in Skylar's mind. *"If you destroy me, I'll simply destroy you. I have a part of you now."*

"No!" Skylar yanked with all his might, but the sword wouldn't come free.

The AI laughed. It was a strange mechanical sound, like gears grinding in cadence.

"You will not bind us!" Filzbalm shouted.

"We're done guys—get out!" Melody said.

As Filzbalm gave him power, Skylar held onto the sword and willed it to vanish, drawing its power back into himself. Something of the AI fought to hold his power. It was like it was trying to convert Skylar into data.

"No!" Del's word rang out. The force of his power rolled out across the mental landscape. He and Astara appeared at Skylar's side. "Back off. He doesn't belong to you."

Its eyes glowed again as the AI stepped forward, then it blinked. Its armor shattered and it started scratching like a human that suddenly had a rash. It straightened and screamed like a wounded animal before it vanished from the mental scape.

Skylar sagged, then the mindscape vanished and he was slumped over in his chair on Astara. He hurt worse than he could ever remember hurting. His entire body felt like he'd been beaten to within an inch of his life, and with the way the AI had tried to convert his mental self to data, he wondered if he hadn't come very close to being absorbed into their network.

"Everyone's shields are down," Melody said.

Solaria was tapping away at her interface. "They blast apart so easily without their shields."

Astara bucked violently.

"Oops." Solaria chuckled. "I guess I should've waited for the killing shot until we were clear of the blast radius."

"Remember that next time," Del mumbled.

Skylar forced himself to sit upright. His head spun.

"Looks like Astara didn't take any damage," Del said. "Let's head back to *The Vermillion*. We need to get some rest and decide what we're going to do."

"That's the big question," Phil said and put a tube of nutrient jell into Skylar's hand. "With the school gone, we've only got a few choices."

"We've got some ideas," Professor Aduncus said. "But we're going to have to talk to the parents first."

Skylar wasn't sure what those ideas were, but as long as he could stay with Del, Solaria, and Melody, he was going to be good with it. They were his family— there was no way around that. He opened the tube of jell. It was clear, odorless and tasteless. The only thing it was, was slimy. Telling himself it was good for him, Skylar did his best to ignore the awful texture. It would help him regain his strength until he got back to the war cruiser and its food dispensers. At that moment, even a synthetic burger sounded good.

21
Reunions

SINCE THEY returned to *The Vermillion* as heroes, Skylar had been doing his best to stay out of sight and hide in Astara. It hadn't even been his idea that succeeded in defeating the AI armada. Not that Admiral Temer admitted it was an AI fleet—he still had his people searching for a carrier wave that must've been controlling them.

Seconds after the Ruby Guard finished off the ships, the stargate was operational again.

Del stared at the main screen and shook his head. "This doesn't make any sense."

"You've been saying that for hours," Skylar said from his seat a few feet away.

"And I'm right." Del tapped the image of the stargate that was an actual, real-time image with data overlaid on it. They still hadn't gotten a proper viewscreen, but they had managed to get Astara equipped with cameras, although the image was coming from *The Vermillion* since she'd tapped into their com feed. "The AI in the stargate didn't appear to be affected by the virus. After Melody deployed it, the stargate was still locked down. We tried sending a message through with no response. Then as soon as the last ship was destroyed, the stargate miraculously started working again. Something's not right in that."

"Maybe it wasn't an AI in the stargate—maybe it was some kind of remote control tether from the network that had it locked down to prevent us from escaping."

Skylar looked at the picture and tried to think of options that would help Del out, even if Del was the smart one in the room.

Del tapped the screen and the image of the stargate rolled backwards. In fast reverse, it showed several ships that had come through the gate, as well as a couple of the Ruby Guard that had left, dispatched to quell a rebellion on a planet Skylar had never heard of before. Del rolled the footage back to the point when the last fighter that had been trying to make a run for the gate had been shot down.

"Now watch this," Del said as he started the footage rolling again.

One of the Ruby Guard fighters swooped close to the gate as it fired on the AI fighter, blowing it to bits since its shields were down and the virus was making it confused and unable to defend itself. Del tapped the screen and the video slowed.

"Here it is." Del pointed at a flash of light that appeared to move from the stargate to the Ruby Guard fighter.

"What was that?" Skylar asked, standing and rushing to get closer to the big screen. "It looks like light. Like there's no substance to it."

"Exactly," Del agreed. "Melody and I have been over this footage forever. Something went from the stargate to the fighter. Data doesn't have to have anything more than energy to it. I've discussed it with Astara, and although an AI needs something physical to bond to, it can exist just as data for a short period of time."

Skylar walked back to his chair and sat. "Like the time it takes for a streak of light to go from the stargate to the fighter. Would the AI be able to take over the systems of the fighter? They're a lot more advanced than what we had when the AI fleet left Sol Three."

"It'll have a learning curve, but it *will* figure it out," Del said. "Astara assures me of that, and as fast as she's learning about us, I've got no doubt of that."

"Can we see which fighter that was?" Skylar leaned forward slightly. "It should have some markings or something."

"We're already working on it," Melody said from her station. "The problem is, so many of the guard's fighters went with the ships that left. Their systems have some pretty good security. It's going to take us a little while to get through it. Once we've gotten through it, we can know which ship was the one the beam struck."

There was a knock on the side of Astara.

"Permission to come aboard," a man shouted. The voice sounded familiar, but Skylar couldn't place it. He knew it was commonplace for strangers to ask permission before boarding a starship, even an experimental one like they were telling everyone Astara was.

Melody straightened and stared at the corridor. "Daddy?" She tapped her screen and her eyes got big. "Mom, Dad, come on in." She glanced at Solaria. "Your folks are here too."

Solaria jumped up from where she'd been sitting against the wall half asleep. "What are my folks doing here?" She rapidly combed her fingers through her hair.

Skylar straightened and ran his hands over his hair too. The Unicas had accepted him into their family and he wanted to look nice for their unexpected arrival.

Seconds later, four people came down the corridor and into the control room.

Skylar stared as Cafpar O'Byrne strolled in, looking everything over with a discerning eye. "Melody, you never told me you and your friends were working on an experimental craft."

Melody blushed as she rushed toward him. "Ah, I wanted it to be a surprise."

A knot formed in Skylar's stomach. Their story of Astara being an experimental ship from school had passed the muster with Admiral Temer, but he didn't want to look any deeper than he had to when he was looking for answers. Somehow, Skylar worried that Cafpar O'Byrne, the head of O'Byrne corp, the largest builder of starships in the galaxy, would want to dig a lot deeper into Astara than they wanted.

"Solaria." Felonia Unica rushed over and hugged Solaria hard. "We've been so worried. After everything that's happened, when we couldn't get through to Stars' End or your Uncle Phil, we just knew something disastrous had happened."

Solaria hugged her back. "We're fine, Mom, really. We all came through it without a scratch." She stepped back and then hugged her father.

"I don't think having the school blown up counts as without a scratch." Aniu Unica hugged Solaria.

Felonia hugged Skylar too. "But you and Filzbalm also made it through just fine, I see."

Skylar returned her hug. She didn't smell like his mother but having her embrace him made his throat tighten. It reinforced that he was a part of their family and they had become his. He couldn't begin to explain the emotions that were running through him, and how much he didn't want her to let go.

"We're great," he forced out of his constricted throat. "Just another adventure, wasn't it Filzbalm?"

Aniu chuckled as he gave Skylar a quick hug. "You really do have the heart of a Pantherian, Skylar."

"It's good to see you made it through, Mr. Mars," Cafpar O'Byrne said, coming over as Melody hugged the tall, statuesque woman who'd come in with him. The woman was an older vision of Melody, who didn't look much like her father.

"It helps having good friends to get you through," Skylar said.

O'Byrne nodded as he put his hands into the deep pockets of the light coat he had on. There was a brief movement in the pocket farther down than his hands could reach. "Friends are always important. I'm reminded of that every day."

"He's hiding something," Filzbalm said. *"His shields are so strong. He smells different."*

"He's the head of the biggest corp in the galaxy. Of course, he's hiding something," Skylar replied. He was about to add more when an odd look on O'Byrne's face caused Skylar to suspect he could hear his and Filzbalm's discussion, so he shut up. The man was more powerful than anyone suspected, and Skylar didn't like being around him. The fact that he'd disappeared on them in the caves on Pantheria didn't score him any points in Skylar's book.

Footsteps came down the corridor, and Skylar looked around O'Byrne. Professor Aduncus, Phil and Ms. Grissom came in. The control room was quickly growing cramped, and without all the excitement there had been the last time there were so many people in there, Skylar found it almost stifling.

"Ah, good, you're all here," Ms. Grissom said. "Flight control informed us that you had landed. We just weren't sure where you had gone."

Skylar knew Ms. Grissom was still healing from him draining her psychic power. She had admitted to him earlier that they were recovering, but it was a slow, frustrating process. Knowing he hadn't done lasting damage to her made him feel better, but he was still going to be reluctant to use the crystal unless it was absolutely necessary. They'd looked into having it removed, but the doctor on *The Vermillion* said it was oddly embedded into his nervous system and was afraid if they tried to remove it, it could permanently damage the nerves in his hand. Everyone agreed it was best to leave it there and let Skylar figure out how to use it.

"What's going on?" Melody's mom asked as she took Melody's hand and walked in a little closer.

"We've made some decisions about what to do while we're rebuilding the school," Ms. Grissom said. "We haven't announced this to the other students and families, but once the Cosmos arrive, we can lay out our plans."

The idea of Connor and his mother in the small room with the rest of them made Skylar nervous. There were already too many people there. "Since we're getting cramped in here, do you think we should move this to the guest meeting room?" There was also the way O'Byrne kept looking around, like he was trying to figure out everything he could about Astara. Skylar's gut told him that would be bad, and they needed to get him out of the ship.

Felonia grinned. "Nothing like a trapped predator to want to get out in the open. I agree, let's move this to somewhere bigger."

Without any further discussion, they headed out of Astara. As Professor Aduncus notified Connor of the change of plans, Skylar stayed with Del and Solaria—he didn't want to be closer to Cafpar O'Byrne than he had to. Filzbalm surprised him by staying on his shoulder and not flying ahead like he normally did when they had space. The Solar Drake was also staying quiet, a sure sign he'd also thought O'Byrne had been listening in.

The Cosmo family, along with Professors Ruff, Malacanty, Glicken, and 'clOrdie'ce were waiting when they reached the meeting room. Ms. Grissom walked around to the center of the oblong table. Professor Aduncus took a place to her right, with Professor Ruff next to him. The other professors spread out on her other side. Skylar still stuck with Del, Solaria, and her family as they went to one end of the table.

Once everyone was seated, Ms. Grissom began. "As we all know, we've suffered a major loss with the destruction of Stars' End. I want to assure everyone, we are working on plans for a new school." She gestured to O'Byrne. "Cafpar O'Byrne is already designing the new academy, but it is going to be a while before it's complete. In the meantime, we've worked out a tentative plan to continue teaching our students."

"You need our money to keep coming in," Mrs. Cosmo muttered just loud enough for everyone to hear.

Ms. Grissom inclined her head in her direction. "That's important for the new school to be built. To that end, I've been in contact with Principal Fuspatula, who, by the way, has decided to step down and take a position with another establishment. He's appointed me principal in his place. What I intend to implement is a work-study program, for lack of a better term. We're going to split our teachers into teams of two, and each pair of teachers will take a handful of students, ones best suited to their area of expertise, or their species. For example, Professor Aduncus and Professor Ruff will be going to Tursipia and teaching our Tursipian students, our stronger readers, and our stronger movers. Due to the skills of both professors and the ability of the Aduncus family to provide adequate housing for a larger number of students, theirs will be the largest group."

Skylar didn't need to ask—he knew he was going to Tursipia. They weren't going to split up him, Del, and Solaria, since she was one of the stronger mover students in school. He was going to get to see another planet, and his friends were going to be with him. Although he was going to miss Stars' End, he wasn't going to have to miss Del and Solaria too.

Filzbalm rubbed his head along Skylar's jaw. He was obviously as happy as Skylar was. If O'Byrne hadn't been in the room, they'd have been mentally sharing their happiness. But that was going to have to wait a little while. He hoped they'd be able to work out a way for Melody to be with them too, but if not, they had Astara and could meet up with her at the Galaxeria or anywhere else they wanted go. Their place in the galaxy was changing, but they had the means to make sure they could control their destiny.

Skylar's adventures continue in,
"Skylar Mars and the Floating Islands".

If you'd like to stay on top of new releases and upcoming work by Drew Seren, please join our mailing list at www.drewseren.com.
And if you enjoyed Skylar's adventure, please leave a review. It's easy and won't take you very long.

Who is Drew Seren?

Drew Seren was raised on a diet of science fiction, both in print and on the screen. He spent many nights watching Star Trek and Space 1999 with his father. Comic books were a main staple of his reading, and then when he was in high school he started reading *Dragon Riders of Pern* and quickly began devouring any science fiction he could, luckily his father had an extensive library at the time. He started writing soon after that, letting writing help him make it through class. During college and his corporate life, Drew spent a lot of time writing to help him endure the mundane things that gnawed at him. Through his twenties and thirties, comic books and science fiction helped him survive. To this day, he's still reading as much or more than he's writing. He's also an avid gamer, playing first *Dungeons and Dragons*, and currently lots of *World of Warcraft*. He's recently turned his attention to writing full time and exploring the vast galaxy through new and interesting eyes.

Stay in touch with Drew through his website
www.drewseren.com

and Facebook pages
fb.me/drewseren

Feel free to drop Drew an email
drew@drewseren.com